A
Harlequin
Romance

OTHER
Harlequin Romances
by ROBERTA LEIGH

1196—DARK INHERITANCE
1269—PRETENCE
1424—THE VENGEFUL HEART
1696—MY HEART'S A DANCER
1715—IN NAME ONLY
1783—CINDERELLA IN MINK

Many of these titles are available at your local bookseller, or through the Harlequin Reader Service.

For a free catalogue listing all available Harlequin Romances, send your name and address to:

HARLEQUIN READER SERVICE,
M.P.O. Box 707, Niagara Falls, N.Y. 14302
Canadian address: Stratford, Ontario, Canada.

or use order coupon at back of book.

SHADE OF THE PALMS

by

ROBERTA LEIGH

HARLEQUIN BOOKS   TORONTO
WINNIPEG

Original hard cover edition published in 1974
by Mills & Boon Limited.

© Scribe Associates Ltd. 1974

SBN 373-01800-2

Harlequin edition published July 1974

Printed in Canada

1800

CHAPTER ONE

JULIA WESTON crouched shivering in the large winged chair. It was her own fault, of course. Listeners never heard well of themselves, and the moment George Mannering mentioned her name she should have sat up and let him know she was there. But even as she had hesitated, Stephen Brandon had replied, his answer keeping her rooted to the spot and making it impossible for her to do anything other than remain hidden by the chair and wish herself a million miles away.

Even now, remembering what he had said, she blushed with agony and shame: agony that he should have spoken of her the way he had; shame that she was capable of being so hurt by him. After all, it was not as if she did not know the sort of man he was. Nine months as his personal secretary had left her in no doubt as to his failings or strength. Indeed her decision to work for him, and the Machiavellian plotting which had obtained her the job, had been entirely based on getting to know his character.

One could not work, even in the most lowly capacity of copy typist at S. D. Brandon, that most select of merchant bankers in the City, without knowing that its managing director, Stephen Brandon, was, as far as his secretarial staff were concerned, an ice-cold autocrat who demanded total efficiency and dedication. But since he also paid an extremely high salary, working for him – even as assistant to his secretary – was a sought-after position, and anyone leaving, or even so much as hinting they were leaving, was plagued by would-be successors all wanting to know how they could qualify for the job.

Julia's opportunity to be short-listed had nothing to do with planning; merely that fate deposited her in a two-roomed flat opposite the one occupied by Miss Maud Mavis, Stephen Brandon's personal secretary. It was a post which frequently sent her home to her flat long after the other occupants of the block were happily ensconced in front of their television sets, and as frequently sent her out again when everyone else was munching their week-end scones. But as far as Julia was concerned, the financial compensation outweighed every disadvantage.

Miss Mavis was taken aback when she first heard Julia say this – they had become friendly when sharing a communal washing line one Saturday morning – but when she learned that Julia's interest in money stemmed from a determination to make her brother's three years at Cambridge as carefree and happy as she could, she set out to help her.

"He had such a rotten childhood," Julia had explained. "It wasn't only losing our parents, but having to live with grandparents who blamed you for their daughter's death."

"How could they!"

Julia sighed. "They knew Mother had a phobia about travelling by car – it was almost as if she had a premonition that one day it would kill her – and she only agreed to go into the country because Nick wanted a picnic for his birthday party. If it hadn't been for that, nothing would have induced her to come."

"And that was the day she and your father . . ."

"Were both killed." Miss Mavis could not bring herself to say the words and Julia said them for her. "I can never look at a container lorry without remembering," she went on, "and my grandparents felt the same way about Nick. You can imagine how he felt about having to live with them. The minute I could leave school and get a job, we found a flat of our own."

"And you've spent all the years since your parents' death trying not to let Nick feel guilty?"

"You can't blame me."

"I don't. In your position I'd probably spoil him even more."

It was this understanding that prompted Miss Mavis to recommend Julia when a vacancy for a secretary occurred in the Investment Department of S. D. Brandon, and realising that to go to the Bank on Miss Mavis's recommendation was a *cum laude* in itself, Julia accepted the opportunity.

Then without warning Julia's real chance came. Miss Mavis was left a legacy. Unexpected, it fluttered through her letter box in the form of a typed solicitor's letter, bringing with it the promise of several thousand pounds and a cottage in Wiltshire. It was the cottage more than the money which prompted her to throw her serviceable felt hat over the windmill, and within two months she had vacated her flat, resigned her job and retired to be a country gentlewoman. But not before she had offered Julia the chance of becoming Stephen Brandon's secretary.

"If you'll be guided by me," she said primly, "I'm sure Mr. Brandon will engage you."

"But he likes older – more mature women," Julia said tactfully.

"Because he thinks they're less flighty. But you'd suit him admirably – if he could be persuaded to take you. It's a pity you're so good-looking. It's certain to turn him off you."

Since Julia had found her appearance turned most men on rather than off, she was amused, though she understood exactly what Miss Mavis meant.

"If we went about it carefully," the woman murmured, "I'm sure we could make you acceptable. If you want the position, that is?"

"Oh, I do," said Julia firmly, thinking of the salary. "Just tell me what to say and wear, and I'll do it."

So it was that she went for her interview with Stephen Brandon in a disguise that was to become second nature. Gone was the thick wavy hair from around her heart-shaped face; its waves were pulled back instead into a coil on the nape of her neck, its confining style subduing the rich, dark red lustre. No make-up marked her winging brows or thick lashes, and tortoiseshell spectacles she did not need successfully hid her vivid blue eyes. Beige powder blotted out her creamy skin and masked the delicate curve of her mouth, while a shapeless tweed suit, a size too large, hid the elegant proportions of her body.

Catching sight of herself in a glass door as she clomped her way – in lace-up shoes – to the second floor of S. D. Brandon, she had difficulty in recognising the reflection as her own, and knew a thrill of triumph when the director for whom she was currently working walked past her without a sign of recognition.

Stephen Brandon accepted her without question. After a brief glance in her direction, he spent most of the time asking her questions designed to ascertain if she was willing to commit herself totally when working for him, provided she were lucky enough to be given the chance of doing so.

At first she was too nervous to do anything other than give him the answers he expected to hear, but gradually she was able to relax and study him from behind the cover of her glasses.

Until now she had only seen him at a distance, though distance had not diminished his striking good looks. But at close range he was even more handsome; his jet black hair and bronzed skin a perfect foil for piercing grey eyes set below dark brows. Only his voice belied his dynamic appearance: slow and drawling, it epitomised the old-school-tie member.

Charm kept a slight smile on his thin but well shaped mouth, though the charm did not reach his eyes, which remained cold and hard. Breeding kept his head attentively tilted as he listened to her, but it did not disguise the restlessness of the long narrow hands that drummed on the papers in front of him. In uniform of banker's blue suit and navy tie, offset by the pristine whiteness of shirt cuffs and collar, he exuded an aura of such strength that she could well believe the stories she had heard of successful boardroom struggles and take-over bids. Here was a man who would be loved or hated, admired or feared, but who would never, at any time, be overlooked.

Not until she was leaving his office was her pleasure in being offered the job diminished by a sudden fear that she would not be able to retain it. To change her appearance and turn herself into something she was not had been an amusing challenge,

8

but would she have the strength of mind to carry it through? Stephen Brandon was not the sort of man to appreciate being hoodwinked, and once she became his secretary she would be committed in more ways than one. Yet recollecting the advantages which the increased salary would bring to herself and Nick, she decided it was ridiculous to get cold feet now. As if badly fitting clothes and no make-up could alter her personality! She was the same Julia she had always been – as long as she remembered this she would be all right.

Within three months Julia found it difficult to believe she had ever had any other job. Though the hours were long and hectic, the work was so absorbing that the time passed quickly, and as she became conversant with the numerous schemes afoot she began to take a personal interest in keeping them on their smooth-running course.

With understanding of her work came appreciation of the enormous strain Stephen Brandon put upon himself, though it was not until she had been his secretary for several months that she fully realised the burden.

Returning from an arduous meeting – the successful culmination of a bitter battle for the shares of a company – he dropped some papers on her desk, ordered her to get them transcribed and then strode into his office.

Following him in a moment later she found him prostrate on the settee, a film of sweat shining on his forehead.

"Migraine," he muttered, anticipating her question.

"Do you have any pills?"

"I left them at home. Haven't had an attack for so long I thought . . ." His voice died away, its drawl jagged with pain.

"I'll be back in a moment," she said and, drawing the curtains to block out the sunshine, she ran from the room, remembering to close the door behind her and flick on the red light which informed other directors that Stephen Brandon was engaged and not to be disturbed.

Instinct kept her away from Mrs. Rogers, the housekeeper

who was not only in charge of the Bank's dining-room but also the sick bay, with its well-stocked cupboard of aspirin, digestive pills and hangover powders. Instead, she raced out of the building and along Moorgate to the nearest chemist, returning some ten minutes later to hand him a pill and a glass of water. Grey-faced, he accepted it in silence, and once again she went out and left him.

Half an hour later the buzzer on her desk summoned her to his room, where she found him in the chair behind his desk. Involuntarily she thought how well the chair suited his personality. Elegant, clean-cut lines; smooth black leather reflecting the sunlight, yet managing to reflect nothing of itself.

"Thank you for your help, Miss Weston," he drawled as, notebook in hand, she sat down in front of him. "You're as efficient in personal matters as you are in business ones. It was intelligent of you not to ask Mrs. Rogers for help."

"If I had, everyone in the Bank would know you get migraine."

"How did you know I kept it a secret?"

"Because Mrs. Rogers hadn't already told me!"

He chuckled: a warm, unexpectedly vital sound. "Did you manage to contact my valet? I assume he told you what pills I took."

"I didn't call him," she admitted. "I just asked the chemist for the latest, most expensive drug he had."

"Which adjective prompted your decision to buy — the fact that it was the latest or the most expensive?"

"Both," she said, and with an effort kept her voice devoid of humour. But despite this, the look he gave her was sharp and questioning, as though he sensed that beneath her primness she was teasing him.

"How horrified he would be if I did," she thought, and said quickly: "It would be sensible to keep a supply of pills here."

"I will. But it's four months since my last attack."

"It's four months since your last takeover bid."

At once his warmth evaporated, leaving him aloof and with-drawn, and making her aware that he saw her comment as questioning his strength. Did he regard migraine as a sign of weakness? Obviously he did, or he would not be looking at her with such cold dislike. Yet why was he so concerned to appear superhuman, almost *inhuman* in his demoniac drive?

Tactfully she bent over her notebook and at once he began to dictate, reeling off figures so fast that her pencil went skimming along the pad. No wonder he had come back from his meeting with a headache!

The human frailty of Stephen Brandon's sickness – even though momentary – robbed Julia of the awesome fear with which she had regarded him. One could not see a man prostrate and not feel sorry for him; and sympathy – however fleeting – left change in its wake.

It was a change to which Stephen Brandon also reacted. No longer did he seem to regard her as a replacement for the in-comparable Miss Mavis – all at once she was a person in her own right, and an intelligent one too.

Gradually he let her attend to more of his personal affairs, and she made arrangements for his select but elaborate dinner parties and despatched the endless supply of flowers, books and scent to the numerous girls who flitted through his private life. She was not surprised by the number of women willing to make themselves available to him. But how did he find the time, she asked herself crossly when, for the third time in a week, she booked theatre tickets and ordered orchids. No wonder he was bone-thin and always testy in the mornings!

"What's wrong?" he asked, coming out of his office unex-pectedly and seeing her expression.

"Nothing with me," she said bluntly, "but there *will* be with you if you don't ease up. You must have spent all last night working on the Matherson merger, yet you're going to a mid-night preview tonight."

"If I didn't, I'd work instead. Don't worry about me, Miss

Weston. Going out with dumb blondes – or brunettes – is an ideal way to relax!"

"I'd have thought you'd die of boredom." The words were out before she could stop them, and seeing his surprise, she was angry at her lack of tact. "I'm sorry," she apologised. "I shouldn't have said that."

"Forget it. You've known me long enough to speak truthfully. You don't happen to know me *well* enough to speak accurately! Beautiful, dumb women never bore me; only intelligent ones do that."

"You're not serious?"

"I certainly am. Clever women are so conscious of themselves – so eager to prove they can meet you on equal terms – that they're always looking for the chink in your armour."

"They can't find what you don't have," Julia said dryly.

"It doesn't stop them from trying."

With maddening superiority he saw no sarcasm in her remark, and she was goaded into saying: "Yet you want intelligence in your secretary."

"Naturally. She is chosen for her ability to *work* for me – not to amuse me." There was a moment's pause, and when he spoke again his drawl was more pronounced than ever. "I divide women into three categories: beautiful dumb ones who make no demands because they're too dumb to do so; beautiful intelligent ones who expect the man to make *all* the running, and plain intelligent ones who meet a man on equal terms and expect nothing. So if I'm looking for relaxation, Miss Weston, my choice lies between dumb beauty or plain intelligence."

"And dumb beauty wins," Julia said, marvelling at her composure.

"Naturally!" He gave her a mocking look and went out, leaving her alone with thoughts that were unexpectedly bitter. Plain and intelligent. His words, though cruel, did not hurt her, for she was wearing a disguise that could be discarded as easily as it was applied. But he didn't know this, and she was appalled at his disregard in speaking in such a way to someone who – as far as he was concerned – fitted his cruel description so accurately.

For several moments she toyed with the pleasurable idea of telling him what she thought of him; then common sense reasserted itself and she picked up the telephone to resume her ordering of flowers for his latest girl-friend.

Had he asked for orchids or gardenias? For the life of her she could not remember; she had better stick to orchids; at least she would be safe. "Maybe *I've* also been working too hard," she decided, and was glad the week-end lay ahead of her – two days in which to revert to her normal appearance. It was amazing how much happier she felt when she looked her best. Not that she had maintained the same heavy disguise she had adopted when first meeting Stephen Brandon. In the last few months she had discarded the unbecoming face powder and was even wearing a light application of lipstick, though she still maintained her unbecoming hair-style and ugly clothes.

So it was with pleasurable anticipation that she left the Bank that evening and stood for a moment on the steps, breathing in the warm June air. A shaft of late sunlight warmed her head and a young man coming down the steps behind her, gave an exclamation.

"Julia! It *is* you, isn't it?"

She swung round and stared at the slightly built man behind her. "Johnny," she said lamely, trying to hide her dismay. "What a surprise to see you."

"What a surprise," he echoed dryly. "Especially since the last time I telephoned you, you said you were leaving the Bank. You also said you'd call me as soon as you were settled somewhere else."

"I've been very busy."

"So I see." He raked her from head to toe. "Since when have you gone in for amateur theatricals?"

She reddened and glanced over his shoulder. But the Bank had already emptied and they were alone on the steps. "I can explain," she said quickly.

"I'm glad to hear it. But it will have to be over dinner. I can't bear explanations on an empty stomach!"

"I can't go out like this," she protested, looking down at her shapeless tweed suit.

"That's a relief!" he smiled. "I was afraid you'd succumbed to the belief that all the world's a stage."

"I'm certainly one of the players!" she retorted. "I'll tell you my exact role during dinner."

Johnny Armstrong could not hide his amusement when he heard the reason for her plain Jane act.

"Not that I blame you for doing it," he said. "No one at the Bank understands his attitude. When you consider some of the gorgeous creatures he goes out with . . . Maybe he thinks beautiful women aren't efficient."

She shrugged, unwilling to quote Stephen Brandon's own reason. "I wanted the job, so I set out to act the part that would get it for me."

"You've certainly succeeded. If you hadn't been standing in that ray of sunlight this afternoon, I'd never have recognised you. But that red head of yours gave you away."

"Auburn," she corrected.

He squeezed her hand. "I'm not letting you drop out of my life again. Now I know you're on the next floor, I'll – "

"You're not to come and see me," she interrupted. "Mr. Brandon would be furious if he found out the truth."

"Why should he? *I* won't tell him."

"Maybe. But he'll think it strange if he finds you hanging around my desk."

Johnny looked puzzled and then laughed. "Because of your disguise? I was forgetting that."

"Well, don't forget it. My job depends on it."

"You don't intend carrying on like this for ever?"

"I might loosen up a little," she said. "But I have to be

14

careful. He'd be furious if he found I'd made a fool of him."

"No one ever has – yet. That's why he has so many enemies."

Julia sighed. "He never gives a thought to them. It's rather a nice quality – not to think people might envy you."

"It isn't a nice quality at all," Johnny said. "He just never *thinks* about people. He's a supreme egoist."

"Then why work for him?" Julia asked irritably.

"Because he has a first-class brain and I can learn more from him than from anyone else in the City. But it doesn't mean I have to like him."

She looked so annoyed that Johnny raised his eyebrows. "Don't tell me *you* like our Stephen?"

"Yes," she said coolly, "I do."

"I can see you've been too long without my company!" Johnny pushed back his chair and stood up. "Let's dance and talk about *us*. I didn't bring you here to talk about our boss – estimable though he is!"

Though she tried to forget Stephen Brandon, being with Johnny only brought him more forcibly to mind, and she could not help comparing his biting wit and sharp intelligence with Johnny's more facile humour and reasoning.

"Looking like a plain Jane is making me too introspective," she thought later that night as she lay in bed. "If I'm not careful I'll end up being as serious as I look."

With this thought in mind she discarded the sensible long-sleeved blouse she wore for the office for a less sensible one with short sleeves and a frilled collar. But frills looked incongruous with her austerely pulled-back hair, and crossly she took the blouse off and put back her first choice. It was wiser this way, she decided. To maintain an act one had to maintain it completely. Even to lower one's defences slightly might make it impossible to raise them again.

The meeting with Johnny, though brief, had awakened responses in her which had lain dormant for the past few months, and she found it depressing to walk down the road and know she merited no second glance. Yet her monthly cheque should surely be adequate compensation, especially as she could dispense with her subterfuge the moment she left the office. But it was in the office where she most longed to be herself, and she wondered what Stephen Brandon would say if she shook her hair loose, kicked off her ugly brogues and raised her skirts to knee level.

Heightened awareness of herself made her doubly aware of him, and she found him unusually absent-minded, as though busy with thoughts other than business. Wondering at the cause, she glanced through his diary and saw it punctuated with the name May-Lin Kwan. She frowned, remembering when he had first mentioned the girl. It had been three weeks ago when a letter from an old friend of his from Cambridge days – now a member of the Thai Government – had asked him to see a distant cousin of his who was visiting England for the first time.

"Heaven spare me from these duty invitations," he had grumbled, laying General Banton's letter on the desk. "Still, I'd better take her out once."

What had begun as a duty soon developed into a pleasure, and in the following weeks he pursued the Thai girl relentlessly, seeing her late in the evening when he could not disengage himself from a business dinner.

"Have you ever been to Thailand?" Julia asked him one afternoon as she brought him his letters to sign.

He shook his head. "I've been promising myself a trip there for years. But most of my holidays are working ones."

"That's very unhealthy," she said severely.

"I agree. I might go to Thailand once the rainy season is over."

"Will Miss Kwan be staying in England until then?"

He glanced up, his vivid blue eyes mocking. "Do I detect curiosity, Miss Weston?"

"Merely interest, Mr. Brandon," Julia said, glad of her disguise.

"I think Miss Kwan's staying another month." He scrawled

his name on the last letter in the pile, closed the folder and handed it to her.

"Do you want to dictate the memo for your ten o'clock meeting tomorrow?" she asked.

"You do it, I'm leaving the office early, for once."

The next morning he was late coming in, an occurrence so rare as to make Julia wonder if he was ill. But he was as sharp and incisive as ever, though somewhat pale beneath his tan.

"I won't be in this afternoon, Miss Weston," he said abruptly, during a momentary lull. "You'd better cancel my appointments."

She stared at him with such astonishment that he laughed, astonishing her further.

"I'm taking the afternoon off," he explained, "and showing Miss Kwan Cambridge. I haven't been back there since I graduated."

"It must be beautiful at this time of the year," she said tonelessly.

"Come now, Miss Weston, you can do better than that!"

"I beg your pardon."

"Your disapproval is too obvious," he mocked. "I thought you'd be pleased that I'm playing truant."

"I am. It's just – unexpected."

"Unexpected things often are!" He picked up the telephone. "What florist do you use for me?"

"Constance Spry. Is there anything you'd like me to order?"

"I'll do it myself."

Knowing she was dismissed, Julia went out, glad to sit at her desk and take the weight off legs that were suddenly trembling.

The office without Stephen Brandon was a lifeless place. Though there was a lot of work to get through she was constantly aware of the time, and kept glancing at the clock as if by doing so she could make it move more quickly. He and Miss Kwan must be in Cambridge by now, unless they had stopped somewhere for lunch. Four o'clock came and with it thoughts of the river Cam and a punt gliding gracefully on the water; then five o'clock and tea, and six o'clock and a walk across the lawns through the cloisters, followed by a leisurely drive back through "the leafy English lanes and into London town." John Drinkwater's poem flashed into her mind and the unexpected sting of tears brought memories of Nick. It was weeks since she had seen him; that was why she was depressed. Even as she said this, she knew she was lying; but sometimes lies were easier than the truth, particularly when it was a truth she was afraid to face.

Preoccupied with thoughts she dared not examine, she made some unusual errors with her work, and at seven o'clock was still typing back a detailed report. Everyone had long since gone home and though she knew she could have left her work until the following day, she was determined to re-do it that night, goaded – though she did not know why – by a desire to mortify herself. She was on the last page when she heard a noise from Stephen Brandon's office, and heart thumping, she hurried to see who was there.

A couple, close together by the window, drew quickly apart and, scarlet-cheeked, Julia went to withdraw.

"I thought it was the cleaner," she mumbled. "I wanted to make sure there were no papers lying around. I didn't realise . . ."

"I used my private entrance," Stephen Brandon drawled. "I didn't think you'd still be here." He glanced at the girl beside him. "May-lin, this is my estimable Miss Weston, without whom I could not do."

"Do what?" the girl asked.

He laughed. "Almost anything! Miss Weston's my walking-talking computer."

May-lin Kwan looked at Julia. "It must be satisfying to be so appreciated."

Since it was a form of appreciation which Julia could well have done without, she had to force herself to smile; force herself, too, to remember her appearance. Miss Plain Jane

Weston could not expect to be regarded as anything other than a computer. Unlike this delicate, dusky beauty who looked as though she had stepped straight out of the pages of a Somerset Maugham short story. Large almond eyes – both in shape and colour – stared out from a classic oval face, while a fine-cut nose and chin and exquisitely moulded mouth echoed the heritage of temple beauties who had danced before the Royal Siamese Kings. And with what grace they must have danced: sloping shoulders supporting regal neck and small, high breasts, tiny waist emphasising the swell of curving hip and thigh. From the tips of her tiny feet to the top of her glossy black hair this girl was a creature to be cherished and guarded, the way Stephen Brandon, so protectively close, was guarding her now.

Abruptly Julia stepped back to the door. "Forgive me for disturbing you."

"Why are you here so late?" Stephen Brandon called her back.

"I was typing the report on Ashworth Mining."

"I see." He sauntered to the Queen Anne bureau and took out a decanter. "At least let me offer you a sherry, Miss Weston. Some small compensation for working after hours."

Reluctant to stay, yet unable to find an excuse to go, she took the glass from his hand.

Sipping her sherry, Julia knew how dowdy she must look by comparison with the Thai girl. Though they had come straight to the office from Cambridge – she had never seen Stephen Brandon so casually attired in flannels and blue shirt – May-lin herself looked as if she had stepped from a Vogue Sportswoman of the Year page, so perfectly dressed was she in white pleated silk with scarlet shoes and a band of similar colour confining her black, flowing hair.

"Have you ever been to my country, Miss Weston?" the girl asked sweetly.

It was a brave but obvious attempt at conversation, for in her sensible brogues and shapeless shirt-dress of unbecoming puce, Julia looked more the type to go climbing in the Lake District or Scotland than to take a holiday in the romantic Far East.

"I generally go to Wales," she said. "My brother and I were left a cottage there."

"I didn't know you had a brother," Stephen Brandon said. "I somehow imagined you being alone."

"With a cat and a canary?" she asked, and quickly set her glass on the bureau. "Appearances can be deceptive, Mr. Brandon."

With a murmured "good night" she went out before he could reply, and alone in her office could cheerfully have kicked herself for being so upset by his remark. It was the sort of comment which her looks and demeanour warranted: to resist it was to resent her whole masquerade; and *she* was the only one to blame for that. "I'm edgy because I've worked too long," she decided. "If I'm not careful I'll end up like Miss Mavis." Halfway to the door she came back to the telephone and dialled Johnny's number. After the first ring it was picked up.

"It's me," she said. "Julia. You wouldn't be free tonight, would you?"

"I'm free any night for you," Johnny said in delight. "This is the first time you've rung me. Have you suddenly realised how marvellous I am?"

"I've suddenly realised how marvellous *I* am!" she retorted. "Pick me up at eight."

CHAPTER TWO

IT required great determination the following morning for Julia to slip back into the role she had chosen for herself.

Yet though will-power enabled her to put on her flat-heeled shoes and thick stockings, nothing could induce her to don the puce shirt-dress, and she left her flat defiant in well-cut skirt and blouse.

Not that she needed to worry about Stephen Brandon looking at her, she thought wryly, later that morning, for since he had arrived at the office he had worked without pause.

Only at noon, when the telephone rang, did he stop his dictation.

"I'm sorry," Julia apologised, reaching for the receiver. "I asked the switchboard to put all calls through to my assistant. I don't know why they – "

"It may be a personal call," he said. "I told them I was expecting one."

Biting her lip, she handed him the receiver and stood up, but he motioned her to remain and she was forced to listen to his conversation. He was speaking to May-lin Kwan and the eagerness in his voice made him seem younger than his thirty-one years. How lightly age sat on him, she thought. Only a man who enjoyed his work could get through the pressures of each day so effortlessly. During her seven months with him Julia sometimes felt she had aged seven years, yet in her employer's glossy black hair there was not one strand of grey. Drat the man; he had no right to be so energetic and virile.

With a start she realised he was talking to her. "It's not like you to day-dream, Miss Weston," he said, and added: "I'm going away for a long week-end and I'd like to clear up as much as I can. Would you mind staying late to-night?"

"I do most nights."

His eyebrows shot up. "I never realised I was such a hard taskmaster."

"Working overtime is part of the job," she said with composure.

"Not to the extent where you have to work late every evening."

"I'm not complaining, Mr. Brandon."

"You never do." He gave a sigh of satisfaction. "You're an excellent secretary, Miss Weston. I don't know what I'd have done without you in the last six months. I never thought I'd find anyone more capable than Miss Mavis." His praise gave her such pleasure that she was angry with herself; as though she were a schoolgirl being commended by her Headmaster! Yet she didn't feel a schoolgirl where he was concerned. On the contrary. Quickly she closed her mind to what she *did* feel, afraid that if she tried to bring order to her chaotic thoughts they would form a pattern that would terrify her.

With a start she realised he was talking to her again: "Your booking to where?" she asked.

"Still day-dreaming?" This time he made no effort to hide his amusement. "I hope you haven't fallen in love, Miss Weston? It would be too much to lose *you* so shortly after Miss Mavis."

"You need have no fear of that. I'll stay here as long as you need me."

He smiled and, as always, she responded to it, though the response shrivelled as he said:

"I was talking about my trip to Paris. I'd like you to confirm my booking at the Plaza Athenée and also arrange for a dozen orchids in Miss Kwan's suite."

With an unusual feeling of depression Julia did as she was told. Yet why should Stephen Brandon's actions depress her? An unattached and attractive man without any commitments, he was behaving the way most men in his position would. It was childish to have expected otherwise. This was an age without sexual barriers; where men and women had no hesitation in showing what they wanted and taking it if it were offered.

But somehow she had not expected the exquisite Miss Kwan to be so available. Racking her brains, the little she knew of Thailand and its customs came to mind: a tropical land of rice and quaint-roofed pagodas, where saffron-robed monks prayed and the military ruled; where women still wore their graceful national costume and considered it a duty to serve the man. But not to serve until married. Somehow she had the feeling that marriage was very much in Miss Kwan's mind, and she was surprised that physical surrender was being so quickly offered. Or was this the best way of ensnaring a victim already fascinated? Not that she could imagine her employer being any woman's victim – rather the other way around.

Arrangements for the week-end completed, Julia returned to room to work; and work he did. Not the first time she marvelled at the dexterity of his mind; the way he saw into the heart of a problem, regardless of how well it was concealed. On this, of course, depended his success: the ability to see more clearly than the next man and, having seen, the ruthlessness to act. For that he was ruthless she had no doubt. He had not reached his present position by charm alone.

Though not young to have achieved success in one of the more usual professions, he was exceptionally young to have reached prominence as a banker, where grey hair and age were synonymous with a senior position. Had he been helped in his meteoric rise, she wondered, or had determination alone brought him where he was? She regretted not having asked Miss Mavis. But her only interest had been in becoming his secretary; knowledge of the man himself had not been important to her. And it was not important now, she told herself firmly. She was just giving way to idle curiosity. The sooner she stopped seeing him as a person and returned to seeing him as an employer, the better for her peace of mind.

But it was hard to maintain this attitude when, at eight-thirty that evening he unexpectedly offered to drive her home, brusquely

23

overriding her protestations that he need not bother.

"It's the least I can do," he repeated. "You shouldn't have let me go on dictating so long. You must be starving." Hat in hand he preceded her to the lift.

Outside the building a silver Rolls awaited him, chauffeur at the ready, and feeling like Cinderella going to the ball, she seated herself in the back.

"I live in the opposite direction from you," she protested. "If you could drop me at the nearest tube . . ."

"We'll have a snack at the Savoy first. I'm meeting Miss Kwan there at ten and Marriott can drive you home after we've eaten."

Biting back further protest, she relaxed in the corner. Kind though his gesture was, for him it was merely a way of killing time, and if, while waiting, he could brighten the dull life of his dull-looking secretary. . . . Surreptitiously she looked at him, wondering what he would say if he knew she was only a year older than Miss Kwan. Yet he did know, she thought crossly, for it had been written in her curriculum vitae. She sighed heavily and, hearing it, he glanced at her.

"You'll feel better when you've had something to eat," he said, misinterpreting the reason for the sound. "We're nearly there."

With a discretion which Julie silently remarked, the head waiter conducted them to a secluded table in the Grill Room where, though partially hidden by a serving table, she was still conscious of feeling like a sparrow among peacocks.

"I'm not dressed for a place like this," she apologised.

"I didn't think you worried about appearances." His drawl was unusually pronounced and she coloured.

"I'm not smart," she murmured, "but I do *understand* clothes."

"That wasn't what I meant. It was just my clumsy way of saying you seem too intelligent to set store by something as unimportant as clothes."

"They're not unimportant." Deliberately she flayed herself.

24

"But when you're as plain as I am, you – you get into the habit of making yourself look as unobtrusive as possible."

"You aren't plain at all," he said firmly, and concentrated on the menu.

The way he suddenly avoided her eyes restored Julia's sense of humour. What a fool she was not to see the funny side of the situation! Self-pity gone, she realised how this conversation would appear to Johnny, who knew her as she really was. No wonder he kept urging her to drop her disguise and go to the office looking her normal self. What a pleasure it would be to see Stephen Brandon's face if she did. But not yet. Nick had another year at Cambridge, and only after that would she be free to do as she wanted. Expectation brightened her eyes and quickly she lowered them, forcing her thoughts to a choice between asparagus with sauce hollandaise or smoked salmon.

"How about a cheese omelette?" he suggested.

Startled, she looked up, realising he thought she was too nervous – or perhaps too lacking in social graces to order for herself.

"That sounds very nice," she said demurely.

"And a glass of Hock to go with it, or would you prefer a soft drink?"

"Hock," she replied. A joke was a joke, but this was carrying things too far.

Their order given, her employer leaned back and lit a cigarette. He rarely smoked and, sensitive to his moods, she felt his tension. Was he impatient at having to while away the hours until ten o'clock, or was he perhaps thinking of the week-end ahead?

The arrival of the omelette happily broke her thoughts, and seeing it in front of her she realised how hungry she was.

"What about a sweet?" he asked when she had finished and, looking up, she saw he had only toyed with his own food. Aware of her glance, he shrugged. "I'm dining later. I don't want to spoil my appetite."

"You shouldn't have brought me here," she protested. "You

make me feel guilty."

"I'd have felt more guilty if I'd sent you home hungry. Now what else shall it be? Fruit perhaps?"

"Something creamy," she said quickly, and then stopped. "I mean – fruit compôte."

The thin lines of his mouth curved. "Don't back down now, Miss Weston. You said something creamy, and that's what it shall be!" He signalled a waiter and within a moment Julia was presented with the sweet trolley and was torn with indecision between chestnuts and whipped cream or chocolate mousse topped with meringue.

"Be a devil and have both," he said gravely.

Eyes dancing, she complied, and for the next ten minutes thoroughly enjoyed herself. Only as she set down her spoon did she realise how nearly she had come to giving herself away, for he was looking at her with surprised amusement.

"It's interesting to watch people eat," he remarked. "It wasn't until I saw you enjoy that – " he waved a laconic hand at her empty plate – "that I realised how young you are. When we're in the office I'm inclined to forget."

"I look older than my age," she said carefully.

"You do," he agreed. "But I assume that's from choice. If you wished to look like the other women who work at the Bank – "

"I wouldn't be your secretary!" she interrupted.

He laughed. "That's true. I can't stand painted women around me."

"*Working* for you, you mean."

He took the point. "Decorative creatures should only be decorative. They're too distracting to work with."

"I'll never distract anyone," Julia replied, making her voice as pathetic as she could.

"I set much more store by efficiency," he said, and signing the check, stood up.

Outside the restaurant, he stopped. "Marriott will drive you home."

"I can manage on my own."

"I'm sure you can, Miss Weston. But why try when there's no need?"

Tears unexpectedly stung her eyes, and hastily murmuring "good night" she stepped into the car.

Driving along the dark streets she marvelled at how quickly the last hour had passed. Though their conversation had centred on business, he had made it so interesting that she had been delighted to listen to him. How immature other men seemed by comparison.

She thought of him frequently during the week-end, but each time she pushed the memory away, glad she was spending Saturday with Johnny and Sunday with her brother.

How crowded the small flat seemed when Nicholas shared it with her, the walls reverberating to the weird, oriental music he favoured, the rooms reeking of joss-sticks.

"I'll have to send all my clothes to the cleaners," she protested, throwing open the window. "Honestly, Nick, how can you bear the smell?"

He grinned and stretched his lanky frame, looking so young and vulnerable that she longed to hug him. Instead she changed the subject.

"What are your plans for the summer?"

"Chap I room with said his father would give me a job in his garage at nights. Then I'll have the day free to moonlight."

"Moonlight?"

"Yes," he explained. "Take a second job."

"You don't have to take two jobs. Anyway, you should do some studying during the holidays."

"Don't worry. I'll get my degree."

He got up to change one unbearable record for another, increasing the volume to make it even more unbearable. "There's more to university than just working," he shouted to make himself heard. "The people you meet count just as much."

Julia remembered this long after he had left in a flurry of

knapsack and parcels of food on his way to hitch a lift. If only there was someone to whom she could talk about Nick! Hard on this thought came memory of Stephen Brandon, his dark, clever face such a contrast to her brother's open, smiling one. They would probably hate each other on sight: Nick's views of the Establishment being those of the radical student.

Smiling at the fireworks that would fly if the two men met, she doused the still smouldering joss-sticks in the sink, dumped them unregretfully into the pedal bin and went to bed.

Never had sleep been so far away nor her imagination worked such overtime. Thoughts of Stephen and May-lin Kwan raced through her brain, each one more intimate than the next, finally bringing her up from the pillows to switch on the light in the hope that light might dispel what her mind's eye was so feverishly envisaging.

But if anything the light made it worse, and her bed leered up at her with May-lin's dark hair streaming across the pillow. How long and glossy the strands would be against the hardness of tanned skin. A picture of narrow, supple hands flashed before her, the thin fingers no longer restlessly drumming on a desk but tenderly caressing soft skin, while a mouth so frequently set in firm, determined lines was all at once curved with tenderness before it lost itself against a voluptuous red one.

With a cry of despair Julia ran into the kitchen, hoping that the prosaic task of boiling water, filling the teapot and pouring milk into the cup would bring her down to earth. But as the water hissed and steamed, so did her emotions, bubbling over till they could no longer be controlled and, uncontrollable, could no longer be ignored. Finally she faced the truth.

She was in love with Stephen Brandon.

Pushing away her untouched tea, she returned to the bedroom. The mirror reflected her troubled face and she stared at herself. The sight of her flushed skin and thick, wavy hair falling dark red around her shoulders – as beautiful in its own way as May-lin's – made her realise the unnecessary despair of

28

her thoughts. Other women vied for Stephen's attention, so why shouldn't she? The fact that she was his secretary need not be a deterrent. It actually put her in a stronger position, for who knew better than she how to hold his attention? How to avoid the things he disliked?

Again the thought of the Thai girl stabbed at her. If Stephen genuinely loved her there would be no point trying to fight for him. But if he was only amusing himself there was no reason why *she* shouldn't try to arouse his interest. It would mean dropping her disguise, of course. How big a risk was it to go to the office looking her real self? No matter what sense of humour he had, Stephen's prejudice regarding the women who worked for him was too strong for him to accept her sudden and total transformation. That meant she must do it so subtly that he would not realise what was happening until it had taken place; in that way she would lessen his anger and the risk of being dismissed.

But what if – when faced with the real Julia – she still did not appeal to him?

"Then you'll be out of luck, my girl," she said to her reflection. "But the least you can do is try."

*

Stephen Brandon returned to the office on Tuesday. He made no reference to his Paris trip, though Julia found it impossible to see him without also thinking of May-lin. It set her nerves on edge, giving her an asperity that rubbed off on her hapless assistant.

"Mr. Brandon's mood must be affecting you," said little Miss Knock unhappily.

"What makes you say that?" Julia asked sharply.

"Because he's in a temper too. He nearly bit my head off when I took in that report you gave me."

"He has a lot of things on his mind."

"More likely one thing," came the pert reply, "and we all

know what that is!"

As the days passed Julia remembered this remark, for he became – if anything – even more irritable. She was also surprised by the absence of the Thai girl from all his engagements, but it was not until a week after his return that she discovered the reason for it.

Going into his office after lunch to put some papers on his desk, she found herself face to face with May-lin.

"The receptionist showed me up here," the girl explained. "I want to see Mr. Brandon."

"I'm not sure when he'll be back. His next appointment isn't until three."

"I'll wait. My plane doesn't leave until seven. I'm going back to Thailand."

Julia tried to hide her pleasure at the news. "Are you pleased to be returning?"

"I'm sad to leave Stephen."

Curiosity forced Julia to speak: "I wondered if you had already left."

For an instant the almond eyes looked blank, then they glinted with faintly malicious humour. "Of course – the perfect secretary who knows everything about her employer!"

"It's one of my duties to know Mr. Brandon's commitments," Julia said stiffly.

"Even private ones?"

The soft voice had a hard edge to it. The cat inside the Siamese kitten, Julia thought.

"Like most efficient secretaries," May-lin Kwan went on, "I'm afraid you spoil your employer. But then *all* women spoil him. That's why *I* decided not to." She turned and stared through the window. Even with the bright light shining directly on her, her beauty was flawless. In a land of fair-skinned English-women her exotic colouring and tiny but perfect figure set her apart. Small wonder Stephen Brandon wanted her.

"Stephen is angry with me because I am leaving England,"

the girl continued. "But it is better this way. For the first time in his life *he* will have to do the chasing."

Embarrassed by the confidence – even though she had desperately wanted to have it – Julia made no reply. There was no doubt Stephen Brandon still desired this lovely girl. If he didn't, he would not be so angry at her departure.

The knowledge filled Julia with depression, making her see the futility of her own hopes. How big and lumpy she felt beside this exquisite miniature. Wondering how long it would be before Stephen was winging his way to Thailand, she murmured an excuse and returned to her office to beat out her misery on the typewriter.

Five minutes before three o'clock he returned to the office, and she heard his sharp exclamation as he walked in and saw his visitor. Then the door closed and Julia heard nothing except the fast beating of her heart.

Three o'clock came and went and though Reception rang to say his next appointment had arrived, she decided not to interrupt him.

It was a quarter past three when he escorted May-lin from his room. There was no expression on his face as he walked out with her, but the flush on his cheekbones and the ice grey of his eyes were sure signs of temper.

When he returned to the office his mood was unchanged, though his first words took Julia by surprise:

"Would you send three dozen red roses to London Airport."

"For Miss Kwan." Julia made it a statement, not a question.

"Yes. And have three more dozen sent to her at Bangkok. White ones."

Startled, Julia's pencil slipped on the pad, and seeing the movement he gave a dry, humourless laugh. "Red roses for love, Miss Weston. White ones to show it can fade."

"So quickly?" she blurted out, unable to stop herself.

"No man should allow a woman to take command of him. Once he does, his life is no longer his own."

He went into his room and Julia pondered his words for a long time. They indicated one more facet of his complicated character. When you thought you knew him you uncovered another layer. It was like peeling an onion, she thought soberly, and hoped there would not be tears at the end of it for her.

Poor May-lin. She had badly overestimated her strength; or perhaps it would be more correct to say she had badly misjudged Stephen's. But how could he ever love a woman if he refused to let himself need her? It was a disquieting question, and one to which she had no answer.

CHAPTER THREE

ONCE more other women filled Stephen Brandon's life, though Julia gained some comfort from the belief that there was safety in numbers.

He was working harder than ever, enjoying the cut and thrust of a commercial world which Julia herself found fascinating. Before joining the Bank her interests had centred on literature and art, but now she began to study the political and business sections of the newspapers, intrigued to see how one could affect the other.

"You have a good grasp of world affairs," he commented late one afternoon during a lull in what had been a particularly busy day.

"I only became interested since I started working for you," she admitted.

"I'm glad you have. I find your opinions worthwhile."

Colour flooded her face and he looked at her with amusement. "It's a rare woman who can blush these days. You're the old-fashioned type, Miss Weston. I thought they'd disappeared."

As a compliment it was too back-handed to be appreciated, and ruefully she bent to her notebook.

"Are you busy during the week-end?" he asked. "I have to prepare a Shareholders' Report, and if I could work on it with you. . . ."

"I'm quite free," she said.

"Good. I'd like you to stay at Forest Dene with me. It will be more convenient."

Julia had never been to his home, though she had heard a great deal about it from Johnny who, with a group of other executives, occasionally went there for a Sunday luncheon.

"It's the sort of place you'd expect him to have," he had

said enviously. "Mellow brick, tall windows and white porticos. He's even got a housekeeper in a long black dress; all he lacks is a wife called Rebecca!"

"Well?" Stephen Brandon's voice broke into her thoughts, "I take it you've no objection to staying at my home?"

"Not at all," she said hastily. "Do I need to bring anything special – clothes, I mean?"

He looked so surprised that she regretted the question; regretted it even more when he said: "You always look fine to me. Wear what you usually do."

As a house, Forest Dene was everything Johnny had said. It stood in acres of parkland, with lush green lawns rolling down to the Thames and peacocks strutting on the south-facing terrace. Unlike his office, which was modern and functional, the furniture here was antique, and her eyes ranged from a Regency spinet in front of a curving window to Hepplewhite chairs set either side of a mahogany bureau; from Persian rugs on well-polished floors to chintz-covered easy chairs around a magnificent Adam fireplace.

After unpacking her clothes in the beautifully appointed bedroom she had been given, she went down to the library where Stephen Brandon, casual in grey slacks and silk shirt, was waiting for her.

"I've ordered coffee," he said. "I thought you'd like some after the journey."

Murmuring her thanks, she took the cup, but hardly had she set it on the desk when he began to dictate. How typical of him to make a thoughtful gesture and then thoughtlessly make it impossible for her to appreciate it.

He was in full spate when the butler announced lunch, and though the meal in the large, formal dining-room was superbly cooked, he ate with such obvious impatience to resume work that Julia did not have time to savour it.

The expression on her face must have given away something of her thoughts, for as they made their way to the library he

34

suddenly veered towards the terrace.

"I'm afraid you haven't had much opportunity of appreciating the country, Miss Weston, but I did warn you I had a lot of work to get through."

"That's why I'm here," she said stoically.

"Even so, there's no reason why we can't work on the lawn. Go and fetch your notebook."

She returned to find him seated in a wicker-work chair and she settled herself beside him. It was a perfect June day, the air scented with stocks and early roses. A few yards away from them the branches of a lilac tree curved and waved as gracefully as a lady in a crinoline, wafting an occasional perfumed breeze in their direction.

Sunlight dappled Stephen Brandon's dark hair and gave a tawny colour to his skin. It made him look unexpectedly carefree and far too young to have so much responsibility. Not that he minded it, she knew. On the contrary, he seemed to thrive on pitting his wits against others. Yet he was far too thin, she noticed with a surge of love, and there was a tautness about his shoulders that spoke of tension and strain. It was almost as though he were afraid to relax, as though he always had to be on the alert in case he let himself down. Was it only ambition that urged him on, she wondered, or was there a deeper reason? Money alone could not be the cause, for he already had more than he needed.

"What are you thinking about so seriously?" His question cut across her thoughts and, lulled by her unusual surroundings, she was unusually frank.

"I was wondering why you work so hard when you don't have to."

"Because I enjoy it. If I found it dull, I'd retire."

"I can never see you doing that. You'd be bored to death!"

"That shows how little you know me. I have many hobbies."

"Such as?"

"Racing, flying, skiing – "

"All *activities*," she protested. "Don't you do anything that lets you sit quietly at home?"

He thought for a moment. "I'm fond of music."

"So am I." She was delighted by his answer. "Particularly Wagner."

"Really? I would have thought he was too intense for you. There's – " he stopped, discomfited. "I'm sorry. That was very rude of me."

She shrugged, hiding a smile. "I know I don't look the type to appreciate intense or sensuous music. But you shouldn't judge by appearances."

"I stand suitably reprimanded."

As though deciding it was unwise to continue with further social conversation, he resumed work, only pausing at four o'clock when tea was served on the lawn: sandwiches filled with ham from his own farm and sponge cakes covered with cream from his own cows.

Julia enjoyed every delicious mouthful, unaware – until too late – of the speculative look in the pale grey eyes watching her.

"You're like a child when you eat," he commented, sipping an austere cup of China tea. "You positively wallow in cream and all that sweet stuff."

"Ham sandwiches aren't sweet," she protested. "They're very nutritious. It would do *you* good to have some."

"Don't mother me," he said idly.

"Then don't play father to *me*." As always her tongue ran away with her, but it was too late to retract the words; not that there was need, for he was smiling at her.

"Right now I *feel* paternal towards you. You look so much younger sitting on the grass than you do in the office."

"I'm dressed differently," she murmured, glancing down at her pale blue cotton.

"It's more than that. I never notice what you wear anyway." His tone was impatient. "You just have a different aura."

Elation could not be denied and her happiness came out in a

sudden laugh. "It's easy to be relaxed in this lovely garden."

"I'm glad you're enjoying it. At least you won't feel resentful at having to give up your week-end."

"It's what I'm paid for." Determinedly she brought the conversation back to a prosaic level. Her plans to alter the status quo between them had been arranged for to-night, and she was not going to have them set in motion before she was ready.

For several more hours they continued to work, while the sun sank lower on the horizon, its mellow rays deepening the shadows which the great house cast on the lawn. It was not until a loud male voice called out that they both looked up to see a thick-set man striding towards them.

"George!" Stephen exclaimed, standing up. "You got here earlier than I thought."

"In time to have a drink before dinner." He glanced at Julia and beamed as he was introduced. "Wish I knew how *I* could get my secretary to work for me at week-ends!"

He went on talking, pausing only to let Stephen introduce him formally as George Mannering, an old school friend from Eton.

He was, Julia thought listening to his booming laugh, a typical public school product, though with none of the urbane charm of the man beside him. But then Stephen Brandon made every other man pale into insignificance. Unexpectedly she ached with longing for him, wishing with all her heart that she could stand close and touch him. Strange that all the time she had worked for him they had never so much as shaken hands.

With a start she realised both men were looking at her, and gathering her wits, heard Stephen suggest she rest for an hour and then meet them in the library for drinks.

Agreeing dutifully, she retired to her room where she lay soaking in the bath and thinking with pleasure of the evening ahead.

The plain Jane image was about to be destroyed and from its ashes a phoenix would arise.

In white towelling bath-coat she padded to the wardrobe and took out the sapphire blue chiffon dress that swayed tantalisingly in the panelled interior. Down with her slow and tortuous attempts to catch Stephen's attention. To-night it was do or die and blow the future! So he did not notice what clothes she wore? Well, an hour from now and he would be eating his words.

But first there was her hair. With a sigh of pure delight she dumped the hairpins into the wastepaper basket and pulled the dark red tresses free, brushing them till the colour shone like dark wine against her creamy skin. Carefully applied make-up increased the length of her lashes, the dark blue mascara emphasising the blue of eyes whose brilliance was already heightened by excitement. Next came her dress, its soft folds clinging to the high curve of her breasts and making her waist seem absurdly small. Silver-strapped shoes and gossamer stockings completed the picture, and feeling like a duckling transformed into a swan, she dreamily floated down the stairs.

She was far too early, of course, but she would feel happier if she were already in the library when Stephen came in. At least she would not have to face his expression as she crossed the wide expanse of carpet. Carefully she settled in an armchair, half turning it to face the window. Relaxing in its depths she was enveloped by a feeling of tiredness. It was probably caused by the tension of the past busy week, she thought, and this final, momentous hour of preparation. Closing her eyes, she let her thoughts drift, glad of this respite before the final dénouement.

Voices, faint and seeming to come from a distance, brought her back to consciousness, and she opened her eyes and gave a little sigh.

"Marrying his secretary?" Stephen said, his tone incredulous. "Thompson must be senile!"

Half rising to show she was there, Julia sank back into her chair.

"Marry for love or money," Stephen went on, "but never because of propinquity! And that's the only reason a man marries his secretary."

Half rising again, Julia once more sank down, hurt and anger keeping her rooted to the chair.

"I never knew you were a snob," George Mannering laughed.

"I'm *not*, I'm being logical. A girl might seem ideal when she's in your office protecting you from people you don't want to meet, but once she's in your home *giving* orders instead of taking them, it's a different story!"

"It might be a happier one."

"I doubt it. Still, I'm prejudiced against working women. I could never marry one."

"There aren't many girls who don't work these days," his friend retorted.

"I don't mind a girl filling in time with a job," Stephen drawled, "so long as she doesn't regard it as her life's work."

"For someone who doesn't like dedicated women, you make a good job of surrounding yourself with them!"

"I was talking about the attributes of a wife – not an employee – " There was amusement in the drawl now – "and *one* has totally different requirements from the *other*."

"Not as far as I'm concerned," George Mannering said. "Your pretty young secretary would suit *me* on both counts!"

"Miss Weston?"

"Don't sound so surprised! She's a good-looking wench. Bet she's got spark in her too – redheads usually have."

"I didn't even know her hair *was* red." There was dubiousness in Stephen's voice, as if he were uncertain that he and his friend were talking about the same person. "Miss Weston's an extremely sensible girl and she certainly hasn't any romantic notions about *me*!"

"I'd like to give her a few notions!" came the reply. "What's her first name?"

Julia was aware of – though she didn't see – Stephen's hesitation. "Something with a J, I think Jessica or Josephine." His voice changed, quickening with interest. "Come into the drawing room and look at the T'ang horse I've just bought. I rather think I found myself a bargain."

Their steps receded across the hall, but not until they had faded completely did Julia rise.

Jessica or Josephine indeed!

Fury sent her racing back to her room. At last she knew how Stephen Brandon regarded her: as a creature apart; a woman who could slave for him and dote on him, but who could never be regarded as his equal.

"I'm prejudiced against working women. I could never marry one".

His words came back to taunt her and her bitterness increased. Did he think it demeaning to regard work as anything more than a stop-gap before marriage?

Kicking off her shoes, she sat down at the dressing table. Even when it was pulled back into a bun, a colour-blind man could see her hair was red! Tears flowed down her cheeks, streaking the mascara, and angrily she ran into the bathroom and washed off her make-up completely. Then rummaging in the wastepaper basket she retrieved the hairpins she had so carelessly thrown away a short time ago and viciously screwed her hair back into a confining knot. Then off with the chiffon dress and into a high-necked black linen. Heaven knew why she had put it in her case. Perhaps it had been a subconscious premonition of disaster. It was certainly a suitable shroud for the death of her hopes.

When she returned to the library she found the two men already there, and hesitating on the threshold, she marvelled at her own will-power in being able to look at Stephen with her usual calm assurance. How surprised he would be if she allowed her emotions to take control and smacked her hand across his smooth-shaven cheek.

Calmly accepting a drink, she went to look through the papers she had placed on his desk.

"Do forget work for this evening," he protested.

"I was checking that everything's in order for tomorrow."

"The perfect secretary," George Mannering joked. "Don't you ever forget your work?"

"I'm dedicated to my job," she said composedly.

"Bit young for that, aren't you?"

"I don't think so. Work is the most satisfactory thing in my life."

Her remark seemed to take him aback, for after giving her a somewhat startled look, he turned to his host, and Julia, enjoying her own flagellation, turned to stare out into the soft darkness of the June night.

During dinner she toyed with the food on her plate – pushing it from side to side and hoping that no one would notice. Both men made several attempts to bring her into the conversation, but she resolutely refused to be drawn, and as soon as coffee was served, pleaded tiredness as an excuse to retire to her room.

But once in bed the tears would not be denied, and she cried for her foolish dreams and bleak future. No matter what she had learned about Stephen to-day – and it was an aspect of his character that had come as a heartbreaking surprise – she knew she still loved him; knew she would be unable to stop loving him as long as she continued to work for him. She must find an excuse for leaving; only then could she hope to resume a normal life.

With surprising calm Julia was able to get through the next day, though she was limp with the effort by the time she boarded the train for London at six o'clock in the evening.

On Monday morning, greeting Stephen in his office and sitting beside him as he worked, she found it difficult to believe that the conversation she had overheard in the library had ever taken place. How could he hold such old-fashioned opinions about women who had a career? Ahead of his time in many ways, it was incredible that he was so far behind it on this particular subject.

"Aren't you feeling well?" he asked suddenly. "You've been

quiet all day."

The telephone saved her from responding. It was a call for him from New York and she left him to take it.

Busying herself in her own office, she was still unable to control her thoughts and for the hundredth time re-lived the week-end. Yet nothing could mitigate the harshness of his attitude towards women who worked, and with sickening realisation she knew that the decision she had made the night before was the only one possible in the circumstances: she must leave him.

A kindly fate sent him to Paris for the next few days and, reluctant to spend her evenings alone, she went out with Johnny.

"You seem a bit depressed," he remarked over dinner in a Chinese restaurant. "It must be having to look at yourself during the day!"

"I *feel* depressed," she admitted.

"Then end the act and return to normal."

"That's what I want to do." The conversation had given her the lead she needed. "I'd like a complete change. Preferably abroad."

"This is pretty sudden," Johnny commented, "but if you're serious about it, I might be able to help you. One of the Bank's clients is going abroad for a year and wants a secretary. It's a Mrs. Rogers – she's a widow – but her husband was an Ambassador for many years, and she's fairly well-known herself as a travel writer."

"Not *Emmaline* Rogers?"

"That's the one."

"Then that's the job for me," Julia said firmly. "I'll go and see her."

The following evening found Julia sitting opposite Mrs. Rogers in an elegant drawing-room in Chelsea. She was exactly as Julia had envisaged, with a quick voice and voluble manner, bright brown eyes and silver hair. Her wit was as sparkling as her books, and it was an hour before Julia realised they had still not discussed the reason she was here.

"One learns much more about a person just by chatting to them," the woman said, reading Julia's thoughts. "And I don't need to ask any questions to know you're exactly the person I'm looking for. Besides, Johnny told me you're divine!"

Julia laughed. "He's prejudiced."

"If you're clever enough to be Stephen Brandon's secretary you're more than good enough for me. As a matter of fact that's the only thing that bothers me. Working for *me* won't be half as exciting as your present job."

"I'd like to travel. That's why I want to leave. Johnny said you are going abroad."

"To Bangkok. You'll love it."

Julia gasped. "You mean Thailand?"

"Yes. It's a wonderful country."

Julia bit her lip. There was no reason why she should be afraid to go to Thailand and she was annoyed that memory of May-lin Kwan should make her reluctant to do so.

"Johnny also said you were a good photographer," Mrs. Rogers added. "If you take any pictures while we we're away, I might be able to use them in my book."

"I n-never dreamed of a thing like that," Julia stammered. "I'm only an amateur."

"*I* was an amateur till my first book was published!" Mrs. Rogers looked pointedly at the briefcase on Julia's lap. "If you've any photographs to show me. . . ."

Feeling like the violinist who just happened to come to the party with his violin, Julia opened her case and extracted some pictures. "I'm on my way to my photography class, that's why I have these with me."

Mrs. Rogers looked at the prints. They showed three views of the City, taken at different times of the day: in the early morning with dust carts watering the roads and the sky beginning to highlight the stark outlines of the buildings; at noon with pigeons strutting the stonework and bare-armed girls in gay cottons strolling alongside sober, bowler-hatted men; and at dusk, when tattered papers were blowing along deserted streets and sightless windows were caught in the last rays of the westering sun.

"These are excellent," the woman said briskly. "Excellent. If you can capture the mood of Bangkok as well as this. . . ." She handed the pictures back. "You simply *must* come with me. I won't let you turn me down!"

"I'll have to give a month's notice. Mr. Brandon might even want longer."

"Well, he can't have longer! I'll talk to him." Seeing the consternation on Julia's face, Mrs. Rogers smiled. "Don't look so worried, he won't bite my head off! I've known Stephen since he was a child."

By the time Julia left Mrs. Rogers she had firmly accepted the job, her pleasure at taking it marred only by having to tell Stephen she was leaving him. If only she could tell him first thing in the morning. But he was in Paris and she would have to control her nerves till the end of the week.

The reality of her interview with him was even worse than her imagination had led her to anticipate.

"If you want more money," he drawled even before she had finished, "there's no problem."

"It has nothing to do with money," she said hurriedly. "I just want to leave England."

"What about your brother? You've always given the impression of being very attached to him."

Trust him to hit the one aspect of the situation which was making her depressed! Bracing her shoulders she said: "I *am* attached to him – too much. That's why it will be better if I go away for a year. By the time he leaves university I'll be home again."

"You can't go!" It was an explosion of anger. "I'd never have taken you if I'd known you'd want to leave me so soon."

"I've been here nine months."

44

"That's nothing! If it had been nine years, I could understand you wanting a change."

Anger at his assumption that her world should centre round his broke the barrier of her reserve. "I do have my own life to lead, Mr. Brandon, and I'm not getting much of a life working *here*."

"If it's the overtime –"

"It's got nothing to do with overtime. I want a job where I'll be treated as a human being, not a computer!" She raised her head defiantly. "And my name isn't Josephine or Jessica – it's Julia – and my hair *is* red – which any normal employer would have known after nine days, let alone nine months!"

The silence was sharp and electrifying, and Julia felt her skin prickle with shame. She would have given a great deal to have been able to retract her words, but it was too late, for the grey eyes gazing into hers were glittering with malice.

"I didn't realise eavesdropping was *also* one of your qualifications!"

"It was an accident. I went into the library early and fell asleep in the chair. When I woke up you and Mr. Mannering were already talking."

"So you listened?"

"By that time it was less embarrassing for me to do that than to tell you I was there."

"You're telling me *now*."

"I hadn't intended to. But you made me lose my temper."

"I never realised you had one. You've always given the impression of being – " he hesitated, "I was going to say calm and efficient, but if I did you'd probably find that insulting too!" He smiled. "Come now, Miss Weston, I'm sure all this can be forgotten. Why not take a few days off and – "

"I won't change my mind, Mr. Brandon. I'd like to leave at the end of August."

The calmness of her voice rather than the words convinced him she meant what she said, for the warmth evaporated from his face so quickly that the words "freezer dried" came into her mind, so hard and cold did he look.

"I'm sure you'll find Miss Knock a very satisfactory replacement," she said quickly.

"If you think so. . . ." He shrugged. "I'll leave you to make the arrangements."

He picked up some documents, the gesture indicating there was nothing more to be said. Unexpectedly dispirited, she picked up the letters he had signed and turned to go.

"Miss Weston," his drawl caught her back. "I hadn't realised the colour of your hair because of the—er—constricting way you wear it. But it isn't red; it's Titian."

His words hit her physically, so forcibly did they remind her of her father: he had been the only person who had ever used that word to describe the colour to her hair. And now to hear Stephen do so – the man she loved, who could only see her as a machine – was more than she could bear. Eyes blinded by tears, she ran out.

Stephen Brandon had given Julia many sleepless nights before, but never one as disturbed as she had that night. The word Titian unleashed a flood of memories that dissolved her composure. Never had she missed her parents more than she did now and, missing them and knowing herself alone, wondered if she was doing the right thing in accepting a job that would take her so far from Nick. How would she feel if he were ill and needed her?

She telephoned him first thing in the morning, and hearing his cheery voice was immediately reassured.

"I've been offered a job in Bangkok for a year," she explained, "and I'm not sure if I should take it."

"You'd be crazy not to."

"But it's so far away."

"If anything's wrong I can always get out to you in twenty-four hours."

She gave a gasp of laughter. How ironic of Nick to misjudge

the reason for her reluctance. Yet thank goodness he did; at least it showed her morbid fears for him had not affected his self-confidence.

With her worries about Nick resolved, if not forgotten, it was only Stephen who obsessed her thoughts, though the obsession itself confirmed her belief that she was doing the right thing in leaving him.

Though he had acquiesced to her departure, she expected him to try to make her change her mind, and she was annoyed with herself for feeling such a deep sense of disappointment when, entering the office, she learned from Miss Knock that he had flown unexpectedly to New York.

"He said he'll be back at the end of the week," the girl added. "Next Monday at the latest."

But one week stretched to two and finally three, and the day of Julia's departure arrived without his having returned. She knew it was probably better for her peace of mind not to see him again, but the thought gave her little comfort and her eyes filled with tears as she closed the drawers of her desk for the last time and walked down the corridor to the lift.

But as usual Johnny was at hand to cheer her up, for as she came out on to the pavement she saw him at the wheel of his yellow sports car.

"I thought we'd have dinner together," he remarked, helping her in. "Heaven knows when I'll be seeing you again."

"I'll only be away a year."

"Long enough to marry a Thai," he said morosely.

She could not help laughing at the idea, but his teasing left her no time to be morbid, and when he finally deposited her at the door of her flat later that night, she was able to think of her future with far less fear, content in the knowledge that she was doing the best thing possible in the circumstances.

Running away might be cowardly, but in this case it was the only logical solution.

CHAPTER FOUR

FOURTEEN hours flying in a silver-winged jet transported Julia from the autumn warmth of London to the heat and humidity of Don Mueng Airport at Bangkok.

Everywhere there was building in progress, the noise and bustle seeming to increase the temperature of a tarmac so blazingly hot that an egg could have fried on its surface.

Expecting the calm of the East, Julia's first impression of Thailand was of confusion; long queues of people waited to pass through Immigration, where passports and visas were checked as though every traveller was a smuggler or Communist agent; crowds pushed and argued to obtain their luggage and touts – offering taxis, hotel accommodation and less salubrious services – followed at her heels like hungry dogs.

Obeying Mrs. Rogers' instructions she stood by the main exit where she was almost immediately greeted by a man in chauffeur's uniform, who explained with a beaming smile – the wonderful, friendly smile she was soon to recognise as particular to the Thais – that he had been sent to collect a "red-haired English lady."

Introducing himself as Chula, he talked non-stop as he drove the large Japanese car towards the city. Like most drives from an airport, this one gave only a brief idea of what lay ahead, though the muddy canals that bordered stretches of the road, and the frequent huddle of wooden houses perched on stilted bases, gave indication of even stranger sights to come.

Most of the passers-by were dressed European style, the men in dark trousers and short-sleeved white shirts, the women in densely patterned skirts that reached to the ground, with tightly fitting white blouses. The young girls sported jeans and cotton sweaters, and had it not been for their sloe eyes and jet black hair could easily have passed for Europeans. There were also a great many Chinese, and though Julia could not discern the Chinese men from the Thais, she was able to identify the women by their baggy silk trousers. But it was her first sight of a Buddhist monk – his saffron robes so bright that they appeared fluorescent – that made her sharply aware she was on foreign soil. How unconcerned he looked walking along the pavement with his shaved head and sandalled feet, a symbol of the past co-existing peacefully with twentieth-century living.

"Most young men became monks for three months before they are married," Chula informed her. "And some of them for even a year. It is the only way to learn Buddha's teaching."

"Were you a monk?"

"Yes. For a year."

Conversation was cut short by the sudden emergence of a car from a side street. It was the first of many such occurrences, for Bangkok, as Chula informed her with strange pride, had one of the highest accident rates and traffic problems in the world. To say nothing of the least number of traffic lights, Julia decided, having counted only three sets as they approached the city.

Once in Bangkok itself she understood why it was called the Venice of the East, for a vast network of waterways, called *klongs*, interspersed the city, their shallow banks lined with wooden houses and shops. Sometimes the canals were so narrow that the tropical trees arching on either side of them, met in the middle, their entwining leaves creating tunnels of verdant green. Here and there a tiny ray of golden light sparkled through the foliage, lighting up clusters of acid pink waterlilies and clumps of orange, yellow and scarlet cannas.

Everybody seemed to use the water as an extension of their home: bathing in it, washing clothes in it, emptying pots and pans in it. But surely not drinking it, Julia hoped devoutly, and remembered she had been warned to eat no fruit unpeeled and no vegetable uncooked.

After what seemed an interminable drive through traffic-choked streets, a fantastic amalgam of skyscrapers and two-storied buildings with tiny, bazaar-type shops on the ground level and flats and offices above, they were bowling along Sukumvit Road, one of the main thoroughfares. Wide enough to accommodate six lanes of traffic, it was as congested as the narrow streets, though the buildings here were modern and studded with advertising billboards written not only in a foreign language, but in a totally incomprehensible script.

With a sharp swerve Chula sent the car through a pair of wooden gates and along a gravel drive bordered by wide lawns dotted with palm trees. At the deepest curve of the drive stood a house far larger than she had expected. Though not built on stilts, it was very much in Thai style, with a pagoda-shaped roof and balconies running its entire length.

Mrs. Rogers was waiting on the steps to greet her, her welcome so warm that Julia felt more like a daughter returning home than an employee arriving to take up a position.

She was led into the house – dark timbered and cool with air-conditioning – and up a flight of teak stairs to the bedrooms. There were four suites in all, and she was shown into one at the far end.

"Each room has its own bath," Mrs. Rogers explained, opening a door to give a glimpse of blue tiles and chromium taps. "The house was completely redone by an American, so the agent was able to guarantee the plumbing!"

"I never expected such luxury," Julia confessed. "I can't believe I'm going to *work* out here."

"You'll change your mind once we start. I'm a hard taskmaster when I get going."

"Is Bangkok usually as hot as this?"

"It was worse a month ago. We're in the middle of the rainy season now, but by November it will be cooler – if you call seventy degrees cool."

"Hardly," Julia laughed, "but heat doesn't bother me."

"You might find the humidity trying: that's worse than any-

50

thing else." A smile crossed the lined face. "I'm telling you the unpleasant part first."

"So I see." Julia yawned, stifling it with her hand. "Forgive me. I must be suffering from jet lag."

"I'm not surprised. I'll send you some tea and you can rest."

"I'd rather try and stagger through the day. If I sleep now it will take me even longer to get back into rhythm."

The rest of the day passed in a haze, though Julia remembered exploring the house, meeting the servants – there seemed to be at least six of them – and examining her new electric typewriter in the tastefully furnished sitting-room where she would be working.

The drawing-room was at the back of the house. Here again a balcony ran its entire length, screened from mosquitoes by fine netting, and filled with lounging chairs that invited you to rest on them.

"There's an active social life here," Mrs. Rogers explained, "and naturally I know all the Embassy people because of my husband. So you needn't worry about being lonely."

"I've come here to work," Julia reminded her.

"But not the whole time. You're far too pretty for that."

"I shouldn't think there's a dearth of pretty women here. The ones I've seen so far were beautiful."

"Thai women *are*. But that won't affect you. Colouring like yours will always attract attention."

Inexplicably Julia remembered how it had failed to attract Stephen Brandon, but quickly she forced her attention to something else. She was in another part of the world and following another way of life. She would not let herself think of the past.

More quickly than she had thought possible she settled down with Mrs. Rogers. After the frenetic activity of Stephen's office, this work was like a rest cure. Rarely did she have more than three hours' dictation a day, the rest of the time being spent exploring the city, either on foot or by car. Many times they were caught in a tropical downpour and drenched to the skin, but this only added to the excitement and made London seem a world away.

Ten days after her arrival Julia walked on to the balcony for breakfast and found a large parcel beside her plate. It was addressed to her and, puzzled, she opened it to find a Nikon camera with several additional lenses.

She was still looking at it and wondering if there were some mistake, when Mrs. Rogers joined her. "How do you like your present, Julia?"

"It's magnificent. But the cost . . . you shouldn't have. . . ."

"I didn't. It's from Stephen. He called me from New York and asked me to buy you something I thought you would like."

Julia's pleasure evaporated. How like him to make a generous gesture and then spoil it by having someone else do it for him. Footing the bill was the least difficult part for him. How much more value the gift would have had if he had found the time to shop for it himself. And he had not even sent her a note!

As though divining the thought, Mrs. Rogers took an envelope from her pocket. "He also asked me to give you this. He sent it to me rather than you, because he wanted you to get it at the same time as the camera."

Marvelling at the steadiness of her hands, Julia broke the flap and took out a single sheet of paper, her heart pounding at sight of the familiar writing.

"Since you believe I have eyes that do not see, I am probably more in need of these lenses than you! But I feel sure you will do better with them than I could, and I wish you well in your new work – and what might even prove your new career.

Stephen Brandon"

The letter was typical of him. Clever, amusing and with the merest hint of apology. It brought him so poignantly to mind that it was an effort not to cry. Picking up the camera again, she examined it as fiercely as if she had never seen one before.

"I expect you'd like to go out and use it?" Mrs. Rogers said.

"Not at all," Julia lied.

"What a poor fibber you are! Anyway, *I'm* anxious to see what you can do with it. Don't forget I have first choice of everything you photograph."

"I wasn't sure you meant it," Julia confessed.

"I never say anything I don't mean; leastways not when it comes to my books. I'm purely a social fibber!" Eyes twinkled. "No, my dear, go off for as long as you like, and don't feel guilty because you're enjoying yourself. Remember you've been commissioned by *me!*"

Too excited to eat much, Julia swallowed some pineapple – sweeter by far than anything she had tasted in England – and set off on her first official photographic expedition. Despite her assertion that she would be perfectly all right alone, Mrs. Rogers had insisted she take Chula and the car.

"You don't speak a word of the language, and I don't want you wandering round the klongs on your own."

"I'm sure it's perfectly safe during the day."

"Maybe. But let's say I'm sending Chula for *my* peace of mind!"

To begin with the young Thai was amused by Julia and her camera. But as he watched her work he realised she was more than a snap-happy tourist, and when she casually mentioned that Mrs. Rogers hoped to use some of the photographs for her book, he set out to help her find the most colourful scenes he could. Julia's idea of what constituted interest did not always coincide with his, for he saw no merit in photographing rice barges overflowing with tons of golden, unhusked rice, nor the families who lived on them. But Julia found one colourful incident after another: a child washing vegetables in a barge's sluggish wake; a young girl combing her long dark hair over the edge of the stern, while her mother busily cooked in a large metal dish poised above a charcoal-burning brazier.

For the entire morning she was busy snapping the varied scenes lived on the broad Chao Phraya River and along the

53

narrow klongs. Despite the poverty and overcrowding, the wooden houses were clean, the people well fed, their golden brown bodies graceful and upright, their faces glowing with a quiet satisfaction that came as much from the pleasure of working their land as from their Buddhist faith which made them believe that no matter how hard their present life was, it was but a momentary step on the path towards betterment and evolution.

At mid-morning rain sent her running for shelter into one of the houses she was photographing. Raised on stilts above the brownish water that eddied darkly beneath, it rose two stories high, the first one being a large room and veranda where the family cooked and lived by day, the second comprising the sleeping quarters – two bare rooms with thin rush matting for beds and the inevitable smiling picture of the King and Queen Sirikit.

Though devoid of what Julia considered the minimum of domestic comfort, the family seemed perfectly content, and as the rain continued she was invited to share their meal of boiled rice and shrimp curry. Warned by a previous experience – when Mrs. Rogers' cook had served them a Thai meal for the first time – Julia was careful to avoid the little red chillies intermingled with the rice. They might look colourful and inviting, but they were lethal to palates used to bland European cooking.

The house was run by the grandmother, whose white hair was cropped like a boy's, a style Julia had noticed frequently. When the rain stopped and she and Chula were on their way again, she asked him why so many old women wore their hair this way.

"It is a sign that they know they are no longer attractive to men. But my grandmother did not cut her hair like that till she was eighty!"

Julia giggled but made no comment. "I think I'll stay out for the rest of the afternoon. Have you got any suggestions?"

"Visit Wat Arun – the Temple of Dawn. It is much admired by all tourists."

It was the hottest time of the day when Julia had her first sight of it. Perched two hundred and fifty feet above the bank of the Chao Phraya River, its majestic pagoda – with four smaller pagodas each side – was covered with a mosaic of small pieces of colourful pottery: thousands of plates deliberately smashed in order to ornament the roofs. It was vulgar and artificial, beautiful and ridiculous, yet combining to form a vision of eye-shattering splendour. Never had her camera been busier, and with the temple recorded on negative, she focussed her lens on the life that revolved around it: the flurry of stalls at its base, their owners shouting to attract the attention of the hundreds of tourists. There was a plethora of objects to buy: copper-ware, reed hats, postcards, silver-gilt jewellery and coloured beads, but she resolutely refused to be tempted. With a year ahead of her in Bangkok she could afford to wait.

Only when she had used up two complete rolls of film did Julia return home, her guilt at staying out so long increasing as she saw Mrs. Rogers on the veranda.

"I didn't realise how fast time goes," she said quickly.

"I wasn't sitting here in wait for you," Mrs. Rogers smiled. "It happens to be cooler outside." She lifted up a pitcher and poured some fruit juice into a glass. "Have a drink. I'm sure you can do with one."

Gratefully Julia took it, forcing herself not to gulp it down.

"Give your films to Chula," Mrs. Rogers went on. "He'll get them developed by to-morrow."

"But they're colour. Won't it take longer?"

"Not if you know where to go – and Chula does. That's one reason he was recommended to me!"

Julia laughed. This was an aspect of Thailand she still found disconcerting; the knowledge that anything could be done so long as you paid the right price to the right person.

"The Thais are no different from other Far Eastern races," Mrs. Rogers said, divining her thoughts. "Corruption is part of the way of life out here."

"It can't make it easy for poor people."

"It's never easy for poor people! But at least they're healthier here than if they lived in Europe. They all have their own plot of land to farm and they can grow their own rice and vegetables."

"But they've no health service or social security," Julia protested. "If they're old and poor they can starve to death."

"Social security is expensive – and Thailand's a poor country. It can only increase its wealth by increasing its industry – and that takes time and money."

"Can't they get foreign investors?"

"Not without too much foreign interference."

"Then what's the solution?"

"You'll have to ask Stephen. He's heading a special Common Market Trade Delegation that'll be here in a few weeks. The Ambassador told me about it last night."

Julia was dismayed at the emotion that flooded through her. What did it matter *where* Stephen was? In Europe or in Thailand he did not live in her world, and if she were ever to have peace of mind she must remember this.

But her thoughts were not apparent in her voice as she said: "I hadn't realised he was interested in politics or trade?"

"He isn't. He was asked to come because of his friendship with General Banton. The General," Mrs. Rogers added, "heads the Thai delegation."

"Are the talks that important?"

"Extremely so. It's not only Thailand, but the whole South-East Asian bloc who are concerned. The majority of them want to have closer links with Europe, but some prefer Japan and several would welcome the Communists."

"It sounds a highly explosive situation," Julia commented.

"It is. So you see Stephen's in the hot seat! Knowing the General so well will give him a big advantage, of course, and he's so clever when it comes to finance that he's bound to find other ways of convincing the Thais that Europe is the best market for them."

"I'm sure he'll do well." Julia could not hide her sarcasm. "He loves using his power. It's all he lives for."

"Surely not? He's always struck me as a most civilized young man."

"Being civilized is much more than owning beautiful objects. It's having the time to develop friendships. . . ."

"He's *scared* of emotional involvement. You can't blame him. He was so badly hurt as a child."

"Because his mother died when he was young?"

"It was much more than losing her. It was the *way* it happened."

Julia frowned. "I always understood she caught a virus and died abroad."

"Diana Brandon was dead to her child and husband a long time before she caught that virus." Mrs. Rogers picked up some embroidery she was working on and Julia, afraid she would learn no more, was torn between discretion and curiosity. She desperately wanted to hear more, but was afraid her interest might be misconstrued. No, she amended, not misconstrued, but understood far too well. Mrs. Rogers was an astute woman who might easily guess the truth if given half the chance.

"I'll tell you the story if you like," the older woman said. "You don't work for Stephen now, so I'm not being indiscreet." The needle flashed and was still. "Diana was a beautiful and intelligent American, a biologist working in London when she met Charles – Stephen's father. They fell in love and got married and within a year Stephen was born. Charles hoped Diana would become the great Society hostess, but she hated that sort of life, and when Stephen was a year old she went back to work." The needle flashed again. "Charles didn't object to her working – as long as it was in England. But he became angry when she began to go abroad. He felt *he* didn't have a wife and Stephen didn't have a mother."

"Couldn't they have gone with her?"

"Charles had his bank to run, and he certainly wouldn't let

Stephen live in some of the places Diana went to. She was doing some kind of research and it meant living in the Congo and the Amazon for months at a time. She was in Brazil when she picked up the virus that killed her. Charles was extremely bitter about it."

"He couldn't blame her for dying!"

"He did. He felt it wouldn't have happened if she'd put him and Stephen first. After she died he surrounded himself with beautiful, brainless women, but he couldn't forget Diana." Mrs. Rogers sighed. "It made him even more bitter about her."

"You make him sound very narrow and prejudiced," Julia remarked.

"To your generation he would be. But he was a part of his era. Unfortunately Diana wasn't. She should have been born today. It was the worst possible luck that they met and fell in love."

"At least she died happily," Julia said.

"Away from her husband and child? She did love them, you know. But she really believed she was on the brink of a great discovery – and she might have been too, if she hadn't died so tragically. But from Charles's point of view, she threw her life away. You can imagine how all this affected Stephen. He was brought up to believe a woman's place was in the home and nowhere else. That she should be clinging, loving and totally dependent on her male master!"

"I know," Julia said, remembering the girls who filled his life. "But he hasn't married one yet!"

"He's scared of marriage. You can't blame him. He was seven when his mother died, and at that age things strike deep. He also saw how unhappy his father was."

Julia was still unconvinced. No matter what traumas he had endured, his present attitude towards women indicated a rigidity of outlook that a man of his sensitivity should have been able to overcome. Surely he was intelligent enough to know that what might be wrong for one man might be right for another? The fact that his father had not been able to accept a wife with a career didn't mean that he himself was incapable of doing so.

Didn't he realise he would never be happy with someone whose intellect was satisfied by a butterfly existence? Not that his choice of girl-friends showed any such awareness, she had to admit in all honesty, for he seemed to enjoy vacuity in a woman, content merely to satisfy his physical needs in their beauty.

What would his future be? she wondered as she lay in bed that night. Would he eventually marry someone because of the need to have a hostess in his beautiful home and a mother for his children, willingly accepting that she could never be a companion for his mind? Or would he – because of his determination never to become emotionally involved – remain unmarried and content with passing affairs?

During the months she had worked for him he had shown no sign of dissatisfaction with this mode of life. Only May-lin, with her exotic beauty, had momentarily been a threat to him. But how quickly his defences had risen when she had tried to prove her strength over him!

Restless, Julia threw aside the sheet and padded to the window. The garden was shrouded in darkness, though behind the distant wall that enclosed the grounds she glimpsed the occasional passing lights of a car. As always the windows were closed against the heat – which even at midnight was in the seventies and filled with marauding mosquitoes – and she rested her forehead against the glass as though its coolness could soothe away her feverish thoughts.

It was two months since she had left London and three months since she had seen Stephen Brandon, but she was no nearer to forgetting him than the last time she had seen him; and now, to make her task more difficult, he was coming to Thailand.

The following morning she scanned the *Bangkok Post* for news of his arrival. But there was no mention of it and Mrs. Rogers did not refer to the subject again.

She had been delighted with Julia's photographs of Bangkok,

and had earmarked several of them for use.

"You've a wonderful eye for capturing a mood," she exclaimed, picking out an unusual view of one of the tree-shaded klongs. "How did you get interested in photography?"

"Through my father. He bought me a camera for my eighth birthday and from then on I was hooked!"

"Why didn't you take it up professionally?"

"It's not easy for a woman. Most news photographers are men and I didn't see myself taking portraits. Besides, I needed to earn a living quickly."

"Because of your brother?"

Julia nodded and sighed. "I've no regrets for what I did. I'm just happy I can be a photographer now – and a secretary!" she added. "It was instrumental in bringing me out here. Thailand's like heaven."

"A rainy one!" Mrs. Rogers laughed. "But in a few days it should change."

Within a week the assertion came true. The sharp bursts of rain decreased and the humidity lessened. All at once it was winter in Thailand: the most beautiful time of the year, when the days were warm without being too hot and the evenings were cool without being too cold; when the sky was the blue of cornflowers and the sun rode across it like a gold medallion.

Mrs. Rogers bought Julia a wide-brimmed coolie hat, and she would perch it on her head as she sat in the garden taking dictation. Sometimes as she paused to touch the springy grass or look up at the shading palms, she found it difficult to believe she was actually being paid to stay here. Mrs. Rogers was more like an affectionate aunt than an employer, continually showering her with lengths of shimmering Thai silks, inexpensive but delightful pieces of jewellery and, more important, evincing an unabashed interest in her future.

"You can't go on being my secretary for ever. You simply must use your talent as a photographer."

This latest outburst came when they were looking at some

pictures of children which Julia had taken.

"If you go on like this," Julia laughed, "I'll think you want to get rid of me!"

"You know very well I don't," Mrs. Rogers scolded. "But when my book is published and your photographs are seen, you'll be inundated with offers. You'll probably even be asked to do your own travel books!"

"I'm not a writer," Julia protested.

"There's no need to be. Your camera will speak for you."

It was an idea which had already come into Julia's mind. Remembering Mrs. Rogers' brief that she take pictures to illustrate what had been written, she had frequently had to turn away from scenes she had longed to photograph. How exciting to do her own book and show what she wanted in the way she wanted.

"I can see you appreciate what I mean," Mrs. Rogers chuckled. "Why don't you start working for yourself right now? You don't have to work for me *every* time you go out with your camera!"

"I'd feel guilty if I didn't."

"Rubbish! You make me sound like a slavedriver. You're too much with me anyway. It's time you were with people of your own age. It's not just a career you need – it's a man!"

They were words which Julia silently echoed. Yet even as she did so, she amended them: not just any man. Only one – Stephen. And since she would never be able to have him, she would have no one.

CHAPTER FIVE

DETERMINED to give point to her words, Mrs. Rogers set about organising Julia's social life, and night after night the house was filled with people.

Bangkok seemed to be the stopping place for everyone going from East to West and West to East, and the large living-room was filled with politicians and business men, writers, professors and the inevitable plethora of diplomats.

Julia was particularly drawn to the Thais. With May-lin as her only example she had been wary of the women, but those she grew to know were so warm and gentle that she found it easy to become friends with them. Though Thailand had been ruled by men for hundreds of years, the women were surprisingly emancipated – certainly those in the middle and upper classes. She was astounded at how quickly they had learned to use their new-found freedom: running factories and shops and following a variety of highly skilled professions without losing their femininity. Indeed as far as she could make out more big business was controlled by women than men; the latter considering it beneath their dignity to enter anything other than the legal profession or the armed services.

Never short of masculine attention in London, Julia was nonetheless overwhelmed by the impact she made in Bangkok.

"It's your colouring, honey," one of the American Embassy men informed with a gravity that came from one Martini too many. "Thai girls are stunning, but one gets tired of black hair all the time!"

"How true!" a soft voice said, and Julia turned to see a man of slightly below medium height, whose own jet black hair proclaimed his nationality.

"Kim!" the American exclaimed. "Long time no see."

"I've been in the North." He looked pointedly at Julia, and taking the hint the American introduced them.

"Julia, I'd like you to meet Major Chan. Kim to his friends – and I'm sure he wants to be one of yours!"

Julia smiled at the Major. "Were you on manoeuvres in the North?" she asked more for something to say than because of curiosity.

He laughed and shook his head. "I am not in the Army any longer, Miss Weston. I am in the Government."

"Thais always keep their military rank," the American explained. "They love titles."

"So do the English!" Major Chan focussed his attention so obviously on Julia that her companion gave a resigned shrug and walked away.

"That is better," the man said. "All evening I have been wondering how to get you to myself."

A fast worker, Julia decided, and gave him a bright but detached smile. "What do you do in the Government?"

"I am with the Department of Trade. But let us talk about you instead. It will be far more interesting." He inclined his head towards the terrace. "It is noisy in here. Would you object to walking in the garden?"

"Only if you can guarantee I won't be bitten. You have the most voracious mosquitoes in the world!"

"They bite us too, not just the *farengs* – foreigners," he explained.

"That's one Thai word I *have* learned," she said, and followed him outside.

Slowly they strolled across the lawn, and Julia, anticipating having to pretend interest in what he said, found herself absorbed by his conversation. Educated in Thailand and Singapore, he had also taken a degree at Harvard, only returning because of his father's insistence that he follow a military career in his own country.

"I wanted to be an economist," he explained, "and I was

angry at having to come back. At the time I had no idea I would become an economic adviser to my Government. I thought I would spend my life commanding a hill patrol!"

"Yet you obeyed your father."

"It was my duty."

"In the West we don't set such store on obeying our elders."

"That is *your* loss. Wisdom comes with experience, and experience comes only with age."

"Not always," she said.

"Generally."

"Generalising can be dangerous!"

He laughed. "You play with words, Julia. I may call you Julia?" She nodded and he went on: "You are a relative of Mrs. Rogers?"

"Her secretary – but she treats me like a daughter."

"She is an excellent woman. More like an American."

"What is that supposed to mean?"

"That she has the determination to get what she wants from life. Englishwomen are too placid to fight. Now *I* am generalising! You will complain again."

She smiled. "Make a generalisation about your own country-women, Major."

"Call me Kim," he said, and paused in thought. "I think they are velvet outside and iron within. That is why I am still unmarried!" He sighed. "It is the one source of argument between my father and myself. Most men of my age are already married with a family."

"I wouldn't have thought it difficult for you to find someone who was *all* velvet!"

"That would be boring! You see I want the best of both worlds. Velvet and a touch of steel! But now I think I have found her."

His voice, suddenly lower and husky, made her aware that she was alone with him in the darkness some distance from the house, and resolutely she kept the conversation prosaic.

"What economic policies are you concerned with at the Ministry, Major Chan?"

"Kim," he reminded her, and chuckled, the sound telling her he was aware of her ploy, though he answered her question seriously. "I deal with foreign investments – both in industry and agriculture. But agriculture is the least rewarding. If we wish to progress we must use our labour force for more lucrative employment."

"Can you do that?"

"Not alone. We must have financial aid."

"From East or West?" she asked idly, and was surprised at his sharp reaction, for he stopped walking so abruptly that she collided with him.

"Why should we look East?"

"Because of Japan. They would be a big market for your products."

"My Government wish for ties with Europe," he said firmly. "And if I did not agree with General Banton I would not serve him."

"You know the General?" she asked quickly.

"Of course I work for him. Do *you* know him?"

"No. But the man I used to work for in England is a friend of his. An English banker," she added.

"You are referring to Stephen Brandon?"

"Yes."

"You must be looking forward to meeting him again," Kim said. "He will be here soon."

"That doesn't mean I'll see him," she smiled. "I was his secretary, not his friend."

"But you are a woman and very beautiful. I am sure you will see him again!"

She laughed. "Do you always find prognosis so easy?"

"What is difficult about prognosticating the behaviour of a man towards a lovely woman? You must know that yourself."

"All I know is that I'm being eaten alive," she said, scratching

65

her arm. "Let's go inside. It's safer."

"Is it only the insects you wish to escape from?" he asked as he quickened his pace to match hers.

"Certainly," she retorted, and from his laugh knew he did not believe her.

*

Kim Chan made no secret of his attraction for Julia, and with relentless efficiency set about pursuing her.

Julia was reluctant to go out with him, for despite their charm, she knew the Thais were a proud race and a passionate one too, and she could only envisage their relationship ending acrimoniously.

"You're being ridiculous," Mrs. Rogers commented. "All the poor man wants is a chance to take you out. He isn't suggesting a week-end at the beach!"

"Not yet!" Julia grinned. "But I've read a lot about Thai customs and I don't see myself as a minor wife."

"Since he isn't even married, how can you be? Honestly, Julia, you *are* a baby! Anyway, most Thai wives these days are too emancipated to let their husbands have minor wives. If a man wants one, he runs the risk of being divorced."

"I should think so too! I'd never heard of the custom until I came out here."

"The Chinese had them for thousands of years," Mrs. Rogers said dryly, "but they called them concubines!"

Julia laughed. "You've made your point, ma'am. Next time Kim asks me out I'll say yes."

Two days later Julia went out alone with Kim, feeling as nervous as if she were dating a man from Mars, and not until several hours had elapsed did she admit how foolish her fears had been. Expecting to fight for her virtue, she had found herself treated as a friend and equal. So much for her preconceived ideas!

"Are you free for dinner tomorrow?" Kim asked as he brought her home.

"So soon?"

"I'm making up for lost time!"

"Tomorrow might be difficult. I'm not here on holiday, you know."

"But you don't work in the evening?"

"Sometimes I do. It depends if we've been sightseeing during the day." She hesitated. "But I should be free tomorrow night. Mrs. Rogers is dining at the British Embassy."

"Then I'll call for you at eight."

He raised her hand to his lips, his gesture again reminding her how Westernised he was. Yet in other respects he was typical of his race, and she learned more of this as her friendship with him grew.

Very much a man of the twentieth century, he nonetheless had the fatalistic outlook of the Buddhist: a belief in other lives to come, which made him able to shrug aside the many aspects of Thai life which she found difficult to accept.

"My belief is part of my heritage," he said one evening. "I cannot change."

"Then why not give up working and just let things happen? If you believe in fate so strongly...."

"Not fate," he corrected. "I believe we are each responsible for our own improvement, and that only as we improve – through prayer and meditation – can we attain a higher life."

"I'm out of my depth," she sighed.

"If you are interested, I will let you have some books on the subject. But I certainly do not wish you to think I have a *laisser-faire* attitude to my people. I want them to have a better life today – not in the life to come!" He stopped and shrugged. "But I must not bore you with politics. Let us talk of other things."

"I'd like to talk politics."

"No," he said firmly. "In a few days' time your Mr. Brandon arrives, and I will be doing nothing else!"

The fork slipped from Julia's fingers and she hastily picked it up. They were dining in a Thai restaurant, sitting on a carpeted floor in front of an ornately carved low table, with cushions supporting their backs.

"Once the Trade Talks start," Kim went on, "I will be extremely busy. The General is determined to get complete agreement on everything, and that means hard bargaining and diplomacy."

"Who will be doing the bargaining?"

"Mr. Brandon, I should think. Our position is so weak we will have to rely on diplomacy!"

"You must have *something* Europe wants," she replied, "or there wouldn't be a delegation here in the first place!"

He acknowledged the truth of her statement with a slight smile which lifted the corners of his small, finely cut mouth. "Our strength – for want of a better word – comes from our geographic position. We are like a linch-pin; the last bastion against Communism."

"Is that *your* biggest fear too?"

"Naturally. I believe in freedom for the individual." He took up a bowl of sauce and poured some liberally over her rice, laughing as she wrinkled her nose at the fishy smell. "You must get used to it. Once you do, you will like it."

"What about *my* freedom?" she laughed.

"I am giving freedom to your taste buds! Or do you only want to enjoy bacon and eggs and rice pudding?"

"You know I don't!"

"Then try all our food. My father will appreciate it if you enjoy our curries."

"Will I be meeting your father?" she asked with careful lack of expression.

"Certainly. It is important to me."

It would have been impossible not to understand what he meant, and though unwilling to have him continue the conversation, she knew that to try and change it would annoy him.

Because of this she kept the subject on his family, questioning him about his mother and brothers and sisters.

"My two sisters are married and live with their husbands' families. Two of my brothers are married also, and their wives live with my parents."

"Who rules the kitchen?" Julia asked with a smile.

"We have a cook and plenty of servants. But each wife has certain duties. They all live happily together, I assure you."

"I find it hard to believe. In the West – "

"There are many things wrong with the West," Kim intervened. "And loss of family feeling is one of them."

"Our people like to have their own homes."

"I can understand that. But lovers can still be alone when they wish. To live with one's parents is a joy that should not be denied them as long as they are alive. If you take the wisdom and experience of age, and apply it with the energy of the young, great things can be done."

Julia knew Kim had again veered to politics, and realised how much his country meant to him. Irrationally she wondered how good a negotiator Stephen would be. Dealing with a Government was a far cry from dealing with businessmen. He would not be able to use money to buy advantages of stock position, nor sway shareholders with promises of bigger profits. All he could rely on was his wiliness to bargain, his ability to cajole and his charm to bring dissidents into line.

Returning home with Kim later that evening she debated the wisdom of seeing him again. Despite his maintained air of friendship, he had let slip a few telling phrases tonight which indicated the direction of his thoughts, and flattering though it was to be regarded as a suitable wife for a man who was obviously going far in the service of his country, she knew she was not suited – mentally or emotionally – for the position.

She did not love him. It had nothing to do with Stephen, she told herself firmly, for she had no intention of spending the rest of her life pining for him! But Kim was not the right man for her.

But the knowledge that Stephen would soon be in Bangkok goaded her into going out night after night, and though she divided her time between several of the young men she had met from the British and American Embassies, Kim always managed to be around.

She would not have been human had she not been flattered by his persistence, and with the *Bangkok Post* blazing headlines about the arrival of the Trade Delegation, and heartbreakingly flattering pictures of a narrow, handsome face she had hoped never to see again, she inevitably turned to Kim for comfort, finding his gentleness balm to her wounded pride. At least *he* saw her as a beautiful, desirable woman.

The Delegation's arrival in Bangkok precipitated a rush of social functions to which Julia was luckily not invited. Mrs. Rogers might regard her as more of a daughter than a secretary, but thank heavens Embassy protocol was more stiffnecked.

Mrs. Rogers met Stephen on the third night of his stay, and returned to the house the same time as Kim was saying goodnight to Julia. Together the two women went into the drawing-room for a few words before going to bed, and Mrs. Rogers headed directly for the sweet dish.

"A poor dinner?" Julia commiserated.

"Typical British Embassy food! And even when it's good – which is rare – there's never enough of it!"

"You just love eating," Julia said affectionately, and took a piece of chocolate proffered.

"Why are you back so early?" Mrs. Rogers asked.

"Kim has an early meeting with General Banton."

The older woman nodded wisely. "The talks are beginning in earnest."

"I thought they'd already begun."

"Only the preliminaries – all smiles and promises but nothing serious!"

Julia perched on the edge of a chair and swung one silken-clad leg idly. "You're very knowledgeable about what's going on."

"We were talking about it at dinner to-night." A faint flush gave Mrs. Rogers an unexpectedly young appearance. "I sat next to Stephen, as a matter of fact, and he sent you his regards and asked how you were."

Julia was glad the folds of her dress hid her trembling hands. "I hope you said I was fine?"

"Of course – and that you were having a wonderful time. I had the impression he wishes to see you. Not that he'll have much time in the next few weeks," she went on quickly. "The negotiations will be difficult, and he also has problems with his secretary."

Mrs. Rogers's volubility stopped as abruptly as a dying geyser, and Julia sensed tangible embarrassment in the silence.

"What have you been up to?" she asked lightly. "You've got a a very guilty look on your face."

"Have I really?" Silver paper was screwed into a tight ball and then carefully smoothed out again. "Stephen brought a secretary with him from England and she's been taken ill."

"Tourist tummy," Julia said. "She'll be fine in a few days."

"Unfortunately not." Mrs. Rogers was still concentrating on the silver paper. "The Embassy doctor says it will be at least a month before she's fit. The whole thing couldn't have happened at a worse time."

"It doesn't sound world-shattering to me. There must be lots of other secretaries available."

"But none of them have top security clearance!"

"Then let them fly a secretary out."

"It would mean delaying the negotiations. The girl has to take the minutes of all the meetings – particularly the ones Stephen has with the General. And *they* are too confidential to be put on tape."

"It's only a *trade* delegation."

71

"It's far more than that. If Thailand doesn't agree trade terms with Europe – and a lot of people hope they won't – then this part of Asia could end up Communist. And if that isn't important. . . ."

"I'm sure Mr. Brandon will find someone suitable." Refusing to give in to the impulse to run from the room, Julia sauntered to the door. But there was no avoiding the voice that called her back and, impaled by it, she swung round and looked at her employer. "Is there something else?" she asked.

"You know very well there is! Don't pretend with me, Julia. You know exactly what I've done!"

Julia looked at her. "Would you mind *telling* me?"

"I said you'd act as Stephen's secretary while he's here!"

The fear which had been trembling in Julia from the moment Mrs. Rogers had begun speaking burgeoned into panic and she sank down on the nearest chair: "I can't work for him again. I can't!"

Instantly Mrs. Rogers was at her side. "I didn't do it deliberately. It happened without my realising it. It wasn't until afterwards that I knew I'd done the wrong thing." She spoke with the quietness of truth. "I was so angry with myself – so upset – that I left early and came home. I've been trying ever since to think of a way of getting out of my offer. But I don't see how I can do so without Stephen guessing the truth."

These last words confirmed Julia's fear and she raised her head. "You know?"

"Yes, my dear."

"*Stephen* mustn't know. I couldn't bear it if he did."

"Then you'll have to work for him for the month," Mrs. Rogers said gently. "There's no way out. I'm so sorry, Julia, I could bite my tongue off."

Julia sighed and stood up. "A month isn't a lifetime," she whispered. "It will quickly pass."

Pacing her bedroom, too agitated to sleep, the thought of working for Stephen again tormented her like a hair shirt.

Logically she knew it would make no difference to her emotions. Even thousands of miles away from him he was still in her thoughts, so what did it matter if she actually saw him every day?

Pulling off her dress, she saw herself reflected in the mirror: pale creamy skin, hair glowing like fire. For an instant she wondered whether to revert to her former mouselike appearance when she met him again, but immediately dismissed the idea as she imagined what Mrs. Rogers's comment would be! Like it or not, she would have to remain her real self.

The humour of the situation blunted the edge of her misery, and she half smiled as she envisaged Stephen Brandon's reaction when, anticipating a prim and proper Miss Weston, he was confronted by the radiant creature she now was. And how radiant she was going to be!

However, fate decreed otherwise, and Julia's first encounter with him was far different from what she had intended.

Awakening early, she watched dawn lighten the sky and green the blackness of the palm trees. As the sun's rays filtered through the leaves she put on a bikini, grabbed her coolie hat and bathrobe and ran into the garden for an early morning swim. Even at this hour the water was too warm to give more than a faint tingle to her flesh, but she swam and dived until she felt pleasantly tired, then came out and sunned herself on the edge, feet dangling in the pool. Wrapped in the voluminous folds of white towelling – dark glasses protecting her eyes and a wide-brimmed coolie hat covering straight, dripping hair – she munched at a large piece of pineapple thoughtfully left for her by one of the servants. A breeze, no cooler than the stifling air, caressed her arms, and she gave a sigh of pleasure. Depressed though she was, it was hard not to appreciate the beauty of this tranquil moment.

A dark shadow fell across her legs and, startled, she looked up. Straight into Stephen Brandon's narrowed, amused eyes.

In that instant Julia was aware of how ridiculous she must look: the bathrobe encumbering her body and the bamboo hat perched atop her head like a plate.

"You!" she gasped, and scrambled to her feet. "I wasn't expecting you."

"So it seems," he drawled, and raked her from dripping hair to bare toes. "I appear to have come at an inopportune time."

He seated himself in a deck chair and she studied him from the protection of her dark glasses. How immaculate he looked in a grey silk suit, his black hair glinting in the sunlight. His tanned skin made him look more of a Thai than Kim, though he was too tall to be anything but British. Aware of him watching her, she swallowed the last mouthful of pineapple and rubbed her mouth.

"I understand your secretary was ill," she said.

"That's why I'm here. I wanted to speak to you about Mrs. Rogers's offer." He could not see her eyes from behind their dark lenses, but he must have been aware of the sudden movement of her head, for he said quickly: "I wanted to be sure you don't mind taking her place."

"Why should I mind?"

"You left me," he said pointedly.

"I'm not returning." She was equally pointed. "It's only for a month."

Again he looked at her sharply, but when he spoke his voice was laconic. "As long as you don't mind, we can take it as settled. You've been cleared by Security. The fact that you worked for me before came in useful."

He fell silent and she racked her brains for something to say. "It was kind of you to buy me such a wonderful camera, but you were far too generous."

"So you said in your thank-you note."

He crossed one elegant leg over another, his shoes gleaming as brightly as his eyes. She had forgotten how piercing a blue they were; one moment pale and glacial, the next vivid and intense – the way they were now as he tried to see her through the protective cover of her dark glasses.

"I felt it was the very least I could send you," he went on. "It was a token of my appreciation as well as an apology for what you obviously considered my rudeness in not seeing you as a woman."

"It was presumptuous of me to have expected it." She turned her head away, affording him a view of her small straight nose and the rounded curve of her chin. "I was your secretary; there was no reason for you to see me as anything else!"

"Secretaries are women too!" The glint in his eyes was unmistakable. "I often wondered what annoyed you most – my not remembering your Christian name or my not knowing the colour of your hair!"

Ignoring his question, she pointed to the terrace. "You must be hot sitting in the sun. If you'd care for some iced coffee. . . ."

"An excellent idea."

She moved across the grass, conscious of her bare feet. It was difficult to be dignified padding along beside him like a wet puppy.

"I've often thought about your hair," he said suddenly, "and wondered why you wore it in such an unfashionable style!"

"Perhaps I was following the dictates of Paul!"

"Don't tell me you regarded my office as a church!"

"To some people it was almost as sacred!"

"But not to you, Miss Weston. Your refusal to be intimidated was your most likeable characteristic. Miss Knock's an efficient replacement, but she *will* act like a frightened stoat!"

Julia could not help laughing, and hearing the sound he stopped walking and put his hand on her arm. It was the first time he had touched her, and even through the towelling she trembled at the pressure of his fingers.

"I remember your laugh too," he said. "I've thought more of you since you left me than when you were working for me!"

"Only because my leaving annoyed you," she retorted.

He shook his head. "I never waste time thinking of people who annoy me. I put them out of my mind!"

75

No comment seemed called for, and bunching her towelled skirts to keep them off the ground, she mounted the terrace.

"I'll have coffee sent to you, Mr. Brandon. If you'll excuse me, I'll go and change." She hesitated. "Will you want me to start to-day?"

"Please. My first meeting begins at eleven. That gives me two hours to brief you."

She hurried away, and not until she reached her bedroom and saw herself in the bathroom mirror did she realise what a sight she looked: lank dark hair hanging in rats' tails from beneath a coolie hat, skin shiny and eyes hidden by huge dark glasses that obscured her small nose. Flinging off her hat, she towelled her hair dry until the colour returned to it. Then not giving herself time to think, she put on a cotton dress the same deep blue as her eyes, fleetingly remembering the last time she had dressed for Stephen and the shame that had resulted from it. But to-day there would be no running away. He would see her as she was and she intended to revel in every second of his amazement. Carefully she applied lipstick and darkened her long lashes with mascara. Then with fast-beating heart she went down to the terrace.

Emerging from the flower-filled living-room she looked like a flower herself, slim and willowy, with swaying skirts around a tiny waist, and hair gleaming auburn on a tilted head.

Coffee cup in hand, Stephen Brandon stared at her as she seated herself in front of him. Quickly she leaned back as she realised that from his more elevate   position he could look directly down the front of her dress.

"I'm ready to start work, Mr. Brandon," she said composedly.

With irritatingly calm composure – for she had expected him to make some comment on her appearance – he began to recount the details she would need to know about the Delegation and its members.

"The talks will be held in English," he concluded, "but in

case of difficulty, there'll be a Thai translator with you."

"I hope my speed will be good enough."

"You needn't worry about that. When there's a full meeting extra secretaries will be assigned."

"I thought it was all confidential."

"The private meetings are. But when all the delegates are present the discussions will be more wide-ranging. It's mainly when I'm with Sirit that *you'll* be required. General Banton," he explained, seeing her puzzlement. "I must remember not to call him by his first name. Protocol is something I'm inclined to forget."

"I'm sure you'll manage," she said smoothly. "I often thought you'd have made an excellent politician."

"Is that meant as a compliment or an insult?" he asked with a smile, and stood up before she could answer. "I must get back to the Embassy. I'll send a car for you in an hour."

She accompanied him to the front door and, as he reached it, Mrs. Rogers came into the hall.

"Is everything settled?" she asked, throwing Julia a wary look before turning to Stephen.

"Everything," he replied. "I don't know how to thank you."

Watching his charm at work Julia found it difficult to believe he did not mean a word he was saying. Or perhaps he did? Perhaps her prejudice made her judge him too harshly. After all, why should she blame him because he didn't love her? It was as illogical as expecting every man she met to want to marry her!

With a start she realised Mrs. Rogers was making voluble cries of protest at learning that Stephen was staying at the Oriental Hotel. "But I was sure you'd be staying at the Embassy."

"I declined the offer," he smiled. "It would have meant protocol twenty-four hours a day!"

"But the Oriental is so noisy. Street traffic on one side and boats on the other!"

77

"But the view is wonderful," he replied.

"That still isn't enough compensation. You must stay here. We have more than enough room."

"I wouldn't dream of imposing on you."

"It would be a pleasure. No, Stephen, I insist."

Dismayed by Mrs. Rogers' obtuseness, Julia watched with dismay as Stephen's reluctance gave way to pleasurable acceptance.

"You can have the west suite," Mrs. Rogers said happily. "It has a bedroom and sitting-room and a small room for your valet."

"It sounds admirable. A secretary and lodgings included. You really are my guardian angel!"

Beaming at the joke Mrs. Rogers went in to breakfast, and going to join her, Julia looked at her with exasperation.

"You've certainly made sure I'm working on the job!" she said crossly.

"It was the least I could do for the poor man. The negotiations will be so tricky he deserves *some* peace and quiet!" Mrs. Rogers sipped her orange juice. "Anyway it will do him good to see you all the time. He might realise how lovely you are."

Not daring to answer, Julia poured herself some coffee. Could Mrs. Rogers be right? It was a question she was frightened to answer; some things were better left unsaid.

At eleven o'clock a chauffeur-driven Daimler took Julia to the Victorian-style building that housed the Trade Ministry. As always when driving through Bangkok she was struck by its visual contrasts: the golden pagoda-shaped roofs of temples and the sports cars that revved past their ancient walls; the middle-aged women shuffling along the streets balancing dishes of steaming curries across their shoulders and the young girls in their tight skirts or tighter jeans.

But once her car passed the armed sentries guarding the Government building she could have been in any capital of the world. Guns were guns and soldiers were soldiers no matter what their nationality. And red tape was red tape too, she decided as she kicked her heels in the waiting-room while her name was checked and she was given a badge which she was ordered to wear the whole time.

At last she was escorted to a large, air-conditioned room on the first floor. The chairs around the long oval tables were occupied by serious-looking men who looked even more serious as the door at the far end opened and Stephen Brandon and General Banton came in.

Julia was surprised by her first glimpse of the man, for knowing him to be a friend of Stephen's she had not expected him to be at least ten years older. Thick grey hair gave him a leonine appearance, and heavy-rimmed glasses hid his eyes. But it was the wide smile that served as his best disguise, for it allowed no other expression to rest upon his face, regardless of how the tempo of discussion changed.

"He has a mind like a razor blade," a male Belgian secretary commented to Julia during a coffee break. "These talks look as if they'll go on for months!"

"I thought we made a lot of progress to-day."

"Because the Thais haven't put up an argument?" The man looked at her with commiseration. "You *are* new to this! The General's just waiting till every point's been raised before he starts knocking them down!"

Uncertain whether or not to believe these disheartening remarks, Julia had them confirmed later that day when Stephen Brandon signalled her to remain when the rest of the delegates filed out at six o'clock. Hardly had the last one gone, when General Banton returned, and sitting quietly in the corner Julia watched the two men together.

Now that they were alone they relaxed, Stephen's serious expression changing to a smile while the General's smile changed to one of attentive seriousness that made him look less of a puppet and more the sort of man who commanded Stephen's friendship.

Occasionally a phrase reached her ears: Communist pressure . . . the Malaysian States must realise . . . other pressure groups are trying. . . .

Slowly she began to appreciate that though things appeared smooth on the surface, beneath it factions of discord existed like rocks under the sea – and could well cause the project to founder.

"The General's in a tricky position," Stephen said as they drove back to Mrs. Rogers's house. "If it were left to him there'd be no problem at all, but he has to make it look as if he's bargaining."

"Why?"

"Because even some of his own party don't want a Western alliance."

She sighed. "And I thought Thais were easy-going!"

"Only on the surface. Underneath they're extremely obdurate. They also have a great deal of pride. It's a tricky combination."

"Why did you take on the job?"

"Even bankers are expected to show some loyalty to their country!"

"Still, if you hadn't known the General you wouldn't have been – " she floundered to a stop.

"Asked?" he finished for her. "Thank you for appreciating my sterling worth, Miss Weston! But you're right, of course. if I hadn't known Sirit, I wouldn't be here. But as I am, I intend to succeed."

"A personal victory again?"

"Everything is personal to me. If it weren't, it wouldn't be worth doing."

Her reply was forestalled by their arrival home. How strange to be entering the same house as Stephen and to know she would be seeing him at dinner and then at breakfast the next morning. Time seemed to stretch endlessly before her and she felt an uplifting of mood, grateful for the days ahead when she would be near him, forgetting the months and years when she would not see him at all.

But when she spoke her words gave no indication of her thoughts. "How soon will you want a transcript of the meeting?"

"As soon as possible."

"There's at least four hours' typing here."

He rubbed the side of his face. "I'd like to read it through before the next meeting – and that's scheduled for ten a.m. to-morrow. I know it's going to be hectic for you, but . . ."

"You warned me I'd be working long hours. It's quite like old times."

"*Some* things have changed," he murmured, and politely let her precede him across the hall.

Her assumption that there were four hours' typing was an underestimate, and at eight-thirty – with half her notes still untouched – she decided on sandwiches and coffee at her desk instead of dinner in the dining-room. She was vaguely aware of voices coming from across the hall, and knew that Mrs. Rogers – with her love of entertaining – had invited other guests to dine. How she wished she could join them. But perhaps it was better that she didn't. Loving Stephen was a weakness she had to conquer, and the less she saw of him socially, the better.

It was after ten o'clock when she pulled the last page from her typewriter and stretched with satisfaction. Though reluctant to go in search of him she remembered he wished to study the transcript before the next meeting, and holding the sheets in her hand she went on to the terrace.

To her tired eyes it seemed full of people and she stood still for a moment, accustoming herself to a darkness interspersed with the mellow glow of candles. Gradually she made out Mrs. Rogers and several other couples from various Embassies. But of Stephen there was no sign and she was on the point of returning to the house when Mrs. Rogers caught sight of her and pointed in the direction of the pool.

Walking across the grass, the warm tropical air caressing her skin, Julia could almost believe she was going to meet her lover instead of a man who regarded her as a machine. But no matter how she tried to quell her thoughts she could not slow the fast beat of her heart as she reached the pool and, in a hammock in the distance, saw the glow of a cigar. She walked across the flagstones, her clicking heels drowning the myriad sounds of insects. Only as the aroma of Havana smoke reached her nostrils did she also smell the elusive scent that wafted her back in time and space to Stephen's office in London and May-lin Kwan.

With a conscious effort Julia moved closer. "I'm sorry to interrupt you, Mr. Brandon, but I have the transcript."

"Good." His voice was matter-of-fact. "You remember Miss Kwan?"

"Of course." In the darkness Julia made out a slim form, darker than the shadows; but there was no mistaking the husky voice.

"I never thought we'd meet in Thailand, Miss Weston – and with you still working for Stephen!"

"Only temporarily," Julia replied "I'm here with Mrs. Rogers." She held out the wedge of papers and Stephen took them and stood up.

"Excuse me a moment, May-lin, I want a word with Miss Weston."

"Of course, darling!"

The words floated behind Julia as she walked back across the lawn, the man at her side.

"I didn't realise it would take you so long to type this," he said. "Nor that you would have to miss dinner in order to do so."

"I had coffee and sandwiches."

"You still worked far too long. I had no intention of imposing on you."

"If I said I regarded it as an imposition from my country – not you – would that ease your conscience?"

"No!" He slapped the papers in his hand. "Work overtime by all means, but not to such an extent."

"You needed the notes and I was willing to do them. It isn't necessary to apologise. You never used to."

"I never used to do a lot of things."

She shrugged and turned away, stopped by his suddenly calling her name.

"One thing more." The dryness in his voice made her brace herself for what was coming, but when he continued, his words took her by surprise. "The way you look now – the change in your appearance – which was the act?"

"You must decide for yourself," she replied. "You're so intelligent, I'm sure you can!"

"My intelligence ceases to work when it comes to women," he answered. "But I'll consider the problem."

CHAPTER SIX

IF Julia had needed to hold her emotion for Stephen in check, the reappearance of May-lin Kwan was the brake she required. Yet her foolish heart still turned over every time she saw him, and working with him day after day reawakened her appreciation of his wit and the sharpness of his mind.

During the daily routine of official meetings she saw him with an air of detachment, but living with him in Mrs. Rogers' house made her so physically conscious of him that there were many nights when she longed to throw herself into his arms. The light of day would cool her fevered thoughts, but the violet shadows that deepened her eyes and the hollows that marked her cheekbones bespoke the physical effort her control was costing her.

"I'm working you too hard," he said abruptly one evening as they returned from an arduous session with the General. "Take to-morrow off."

"I intend to," she said dryly. "It's Saturday!"

"Good lord, so it is!" His surprise was so comical that she laughed. "I like your laugh," he said. "I always noticed it even when you were. . . ."

"Plain Jane?"

"Yes. Though now, of course, you're beautiful Julia."

It was the first time he had spoken her name, and hearing it brought tears to her eyes. Abruptly she mounted the stairs, sensing – without having to turn round – that he remained in the hall watching her until she disappeared from sight.

She dressed for dinner with more than usual care, masking her fatigue with rouge and blotting out the shadows under her eyes with pale foundation. The heavier make-up made her look more sophisticated, and on an impulse she changed her hairstyle, piling it smoothly on top of her head and letting a few tendrils escape to curl on the nape of her neck. Her dress was one of the many which Mrs. Rogers had generously bought her: a shimmering sheath of turquoise blue which gave subtle indication of the supple line of her hips and the sharp, upward thrust of her breasts. Completely covered by silk she appeared almost devoid of any other garment, and looking at herself in the mirror wondered whether to change into something less revealing. Then with a shake of her head she decided against it and went downstairs.

As usual there was a dinner party, and to-night Kim and May-lin were among the guests. Glancing at the seating arrangements Julia saw that the girl was placed next to Stephen, and she resisted the urge to switch cards and put her beside a rich but obese French publisher who was trying to get the rights to Mrs. Rogers' next book.

Hurrying out before she succumbed to the temptation, she entered the living-room to find Stephen already there, immaculate as ever in a white dinner jacket. He was pouring himself a drink and slowly turned to look at her. As always when he did so, her heart began to pound, and she hoped it was not visible through the fragile material of her dress.

"Sherry or whisky?" he asked, but before she could reply, said: "No – that dress calls for champagne!" Turning to a silver ice bucket, he withdrew a gold-topped bottle. A cork popped and amber fluid bubbled into two glasses. He handed her one and raised his own in a toast.

Side by side they stood and sipped, and Julia's awareness of him was magnified by their closeness: the tang of his after-shave lotion, the crisp white of cuffs around sinewy wrists and the slender fingers moving along the stem of the crystal goblet as though it were a body.

"Your disguise suits you," he said abruptly.

"My disguise?"

"Yes. I've decided the way you *used* to look is the real you. You're surprised at my saying that, I suppose?"

"A little."

"It's your own fault. You must have made a bigger impact on me as prim Miss Weston than I'd realised."

Not sure what he meant, she remained silent.

"Whenever I used to think of you," he continued, "after you left me, I mean, I always remembered you as the stiff-necked little martinet who ruled me with a rod of iron."

"I did no such thing!"

"On the contrary. I know you were angry with me because I didn't see you the way George Mannering did, but I was paying you a compliment by *not* doing so. To me you were a brain – an intelligent human being with whom I could communicate – not a glamorous body and a lovely pair of legs. Those come by the dozen."

Face flaming, she avoided his eyes. Many times she had envisaged the moment when he would apologise to her; when he would find an excuse for that dreadful, face-losing session in the library. But never in her wildest dreams had she imagined him saying anything like this.

"Now I've annoyed you again," he said slowly. "I didn't intend to."

"You haven't annoyed me at all. You've paid me a compliment and I appreciate it."

"Do you?" His eyes looked into hers. "I notice the body and the legs too. In that dress it would be difficult not to!"

The arrival of other guests saved her from comment and she moved quickly away from him. She must not read more into his words than he meant. Since Mrs. Rogers had told her so much about his past she could appreciate the implication of what he had said, and wondered whether he himself realised it. Refusing to have a relationship with a woman who was clever or intelligent, he had nonetheless admitted to a closeness of mind with her which he had enjoyed and not fought against. Yet like a fool she had thrown it away. Because he had not seen her with the lascivious eyes of a George Mannering she had left him and flown half way round the world to forget him. If only the conversation to-night had taken place four months ago, how different her life could have been. But to think this was to delude herself. Even if she had remained with Stephen he would never have seen her as anything other than a friend. The very fact that he preferred her as the staid girl who had worked for him, and not as her own more vivid self indicated the complexity of his character and the deep-seated fears – and scars – caused by his mother's behaviour. Not until he came to terms with this would he be able to love a woman who was both intelligent *and* beautiful. Beauty alone he could control, and intelligence by itself he could contend with; but when the two came together they formed a combination which could enslave him – as they had done his father – and this was something he still desperately fought against.

Kim's arrival was a welcome diversion from her thoughts, and she greeted him with more than usual warmth, not sure whether she did so to boost her pride or because she knew Stephen was watching them.

"It's ages since I've seen you," she smiled.

"That is *your* fault. Each time I have called you, you were busy."

"Blame the conference. You know as much about it as I do!"

"I doubt that. As Mr. Brandon's secretary you know more than anyone else."

"All I do is sit in the corner in case I'm needed."

"You should learn to lip-read!"

She laughed, "It wouldn't be worth the effort."

"Not even to hear all the secret agreements?"

"What makes you think they're secret?" she chided.

"Because the General is playing a dangerous game," Kim said, suddenly serious. "Many of our people do not want this alliance. They resent Westerners – white men . . . ."

Julia could not hide her surprise. "I never thought Thais resented foreigners!"

Kim sighed. "For many years before the war, South-East Asia was dominated by white men. *We* weren't, but we saw it happen all around us and vowed not to let it happen here. We welcome Westerners as equals – but never on any other terms. That is why the General is such a tough negotiator. He won't allow Europe to dominate us."

On the verge of taking up Kim's use of the word domination, she decided against it, and kept the rest of their conversation as non-political as she could, though she made a mental note to mention what he had said to Stephen.

Dinner was the usual resplendent affair. Course followed perfect course: a subtle mixture of European and Thai food that had required endless patience on Mrs. Rogers' part to produce. Though there was no shortage of servants – so many were available that there was not even need for a domestic agency – it took great effort to train them in European ways. This particularly applied to food, for Thai cooks were happiest preparing Thai meals which, though flavourful, became surprisingly monotonous to Western palates. How tasty a Wiener Schnitzel was after endless hot sauces and plain boiled rice, while a whole roasted chicken had a succulence undreamed-of after weeks of eating it in tiny morsels fried and served with hot pepper or garlic sauce!

However, Julia's pleasure in the meal was dampened by seeing Stephen's attentiveness to May-lin. The girl looked particularly beautiful in a Thai-style dress, the long tight skirt and figure-fitting jacket as revealing as Julia's own, though with a classical severity that made it even more provocative. May-lin was also wearing her hair on top of her head, the glossy black curls held in position by glittering diamond combs. Real diamonds, Julia knew, seeing the blue-white flash, and wondered suddenly about the girl's background.

"I didn't think unmarried Thai women went out unescorted," she murmured to Kim.

"Miss Kwan makes her own rules. The aristocracy generally do."

"*Is* she aristocratic?"

"Her family was one of the most renowned in Thailand."

"Was?"

He nodded. "Two of her brothers were killed fighting in the North – they were in our army – and the third one died in a racing accident in Peru. It broke Colonel Kwan's heart and he never recovered from the shock. He died a few months afterwards. Miss Kwan is the last of her line. That is why she must choose wisely when she marries. She has a great deal to offer."

"You mean financially?"

Kim's shoulders lifted "That too, but I was thinking of her family heritage."

"How well do *you* know her?" Julia asked mischievously, and was rewarded by seeing Kim's almond-shaped eyes flash.

"Well enough to know we wouldn't be happy together! Not even for my career would I wish to be her husband."

"She's extremely beautiful!"

"Many of our women are," he said calmly. "We discussed *that* subject at our first meeting! But she is not my type." He leaned closer, his shoulders blocking Julia's view of the rest of the table. "Now *you* are. You are soft and more feminine – the hardness is only on the surface."

Pleased and also embarrassed, she turned away and from the corner of her eye saw a servant looking at her anxiously from the doorway. Wondering what crisis had arisen, she excused herself and went out to him.

"Man to see you," he hissed. "In sitting-room. He say big surprise."

Mystified, Julia hurried across the hall, and opening the door was engulfed by a cotton shirt smelling of the dust and sweat of travel.

"Nick!" she gasped, and drew back to look at her brother's

nut-brown face. "How did you get here? And why didn't you let me know?"

"I wanted to surprise you." He rubbed the wispy beard sprouting on his chin. "One of the chaps at college was taken ill and his family asked him to fly back home for Christmas. They wanted someone to go with him, so he chose me."

"What luck!"

"Just my charm," he said modestly, and hugged her again. "Anyway, it got me to Singapore – where Jakri lives – and I hitched from there."

"You look like it!"

"I could do with a bath," he admitted.

"Come upstairs and use mine."

"Will there be somewhere for me to doss down? The carpet in your room would suit me fine."

"Don't be silly. We can find a bed for you."

Knowing she could rely on Mrs. Rogers' warmheartedness, Julia left Nick happily splashing in her bathroom and went back to the dining-room before her absence would be noticed.

With the serving of dessert – several concoctions to suit all palates – from sticky coconut and glutinous rice to tropical fruits and sorbets – she was able to slip away from her seat again and tell Mrs. Rogers what had happened.

"What a marvellous Christmas present for you," the woman exclaimed. "Where is he now?"

"In the hall," Julia said, glimpsing a thin figure hovering outside the dining-room door.

"Bring him in."

"I'd like to see about a meal for him first. And he isn't really dressed for a party."

"What nonsense!"

Pushing back her chair, Mrs. Rogers followed Julia into the hall and stared at Nick with unconcealed curiosity. Pink and shining after his bath, he looked like a well-laundered baby, the straggling beard on his chin as soft as down. From somewhere in the recesses of his haversack he had unearthed fresh jeans and a shirt which though full of creases, was clean and white.

"So you're Julia's brother," Mrs. Rogers smiled. "I'd have known you anywhere."

Nick gave her his warmest smile. "I hope you don't mind my barging in on you like this?"

"It's a pleasure. As soon as you've had something to eat you must come and meet my other guests."

Nick looked at Julia. "If you could just show me where the kitchen is, I can fix myself a meal. I don't want to take you away from the party."

She laughed. "You're not. And you needn't worry about fixing your meals. There's no shortage of help out here!"

Catching him by the arm, she led him to the sitting-room where a laden tray had been set beside her typewriter.

"You're looking very haute couture," Nick said as he began to eat.

"Don't let the dress fool you. At the moment I'm very much a working girl."

Briefly she told him of Stephen Brandon's arrival in Bangkok and her work for him, and unaware of why she had left him in the first place, Nick accepted it without comment.

"I'll leave you to finish eating," she said. "I've got *my* work to do."

"Hostess to rich tycoons?" he grinned.

"Dispenser of coffee," she grinned back, and walked out.

She was doing exactly that when Stephen Brandon came over to her.

"So your brother's here," he said casually.

"Who told you?"

"Mrs. Rogers. I noticed the fuss going on at dinner and wondered if anything was wrong."

She was surprised by his perception; he had seemed so engrossed with May-lin she had assumed he wouldn't have noticed anything else.

"I gather he's your pet chick," he went on.

She half smiled and handed him a cup of coffee. Their fingers met briefly and it was as though she had touched a live electric wire. But the current was entirely one way, for he leaned imperturbably against the wall and stirred the liquid with his spoon.

"You're very friendly with Major Chan."

"He's acted as my guide since I've been here."

"Only a guide?"

She looked him squarely in the face. "What's that supposed to mean?"

"Merely a warning. European women are greatly admired here and it wouldn't be difficult for you to get married."

"Well?"

"Don't. Not to a Thai."

"That's a very prejudiced thing to say."

"Don't confuse logic with prejudice." His drawl was sharpened by irritation. "There are too many differences in outlook. Mixed marriages have a high failure rate. It's difficult enough when there's only a difference of religion, but when it's race as well...."

"Surely it depends on the individual?"

"You're one individual I know well enough to advise."

"You might be in need of advice yourself," she said. "Mixed marriages are mixed whether you look at it from the man's point of view or the woman's!"

The bunching of the muscles in Stephen Brandon's neck told Julia that her words had hit home, but he made no comment and, setting down his empty coffee cup, moved back to sit by May-lin's side.

Trembling with anger, Julia finished serving the coffee and made sure everyone had liqueurs or brandy. It was an effort to maintain her poise, and Nick's entry gave her a welcome chance to retreat to the side of the room and sit down unobserved.

Compared with the sophisticated guests he looked young and

defenceless, but pride swelled in her as she saw how easily he answered the questions flung at him, recounting with humour some of the incidents of his journey.

It was strange how one young boy could act like a catalyst on this well-fed, well-dressed throng. It was as though the sharpness of his personality was acid, melting away surface pretensions to disclose the real characters beneath. Memories long dormant were awakened, and youthful aspirations – long forgotten – stirred afresh, fired by the enthusiasm of a twenty-year-old who believed that faith in the goodness of people could dissolve all the problems of the world.

"If I had my life again," the obese French publisher said, "I would be a farmer like my father. He died a happy and contented eighty-eight. Me – " he looked at his paunch – "I will die rich and unhappy at fifty-eight!"

"It's not too late to switch careers," a tall American said. "I was a chemical analyst before I went into the Diplomatic Service, but hearing young Nick talk, I could give it all up and become a revolutionary!"

"I don't advocate revolution," Nick replied. "But sometimes the only way to get what you want is to fight for it."

"There are some kinds of progress you can't fight for." Stephen entered the conversation unexpectedly. "Sometimes events have to happen in their own time."

"Not if it's going to take a lifetime!"

"Even if it takes *two* lifetimes!"

Nick reddened angrily, but before he could speak Kim changed the direction of the conversation.

"Young people like to fight – it's part of their aggression. They all have the urge to pit themselves against authority – to prove their courage. But such desires mellow with age."

"It hasn't with *me*," Stephen said.

He looked so unlike the aggressive, 'I hate authority' young man Kim had just described that there was a murmur of amusement. But he ignored it and spoke again.

"Like our French friend, I would also change my life if I could have it over again. But I wouldn't be a farmer. I'd be a spy."

The amusement of his listeners changed to incredulity, voiced by Mrs. Rogers' exclamation of disbelief.

"You'd never stick it. You'd have to obey orders!"

"I wasn't thinking of spying for my country," Stephen said, "but for industry."

"You mean selling General Motors' secrets to Ford?" the American questioned. "You could make a fortune out of that!"

"And when you have your fortune," the French publisher said, "you would grow fat and retire!"

"I wouldn't be doing it for the money," Stephen replied. "It's the excitement – the danger – that intrigues me."

"Nothing blunts the urge for excitement more than money, once you are rich you like to do things the easy way." The Frenchman patted his paunch. "I speak from experience."

"So do I," Stephen replied.

"I'm sure you've heard of S. D. Brandon?" Mrs. Rogers did her duty as hostess.

"The merchant bank?" the Frenchman said. "I am sorry, my friend. I did not realise you were the banker."

"While I'm here I'm a diplomat – I hope!" There was more laughter and when it died, Stephen continued: "I've more than enough money for my personal needs, but I still have the urge for excitement – the desire to prove myself. To pit my wits against other people."

"You do that all the time in London," May-lin said.

"I wasn't thinking of normal business. That doesn't excite me any more."

"What's more exciting than winning or losing a fortune?" the American asked.

"Winning or losing your reputation," Stephen answered slowly. "That is *real* danger."

"I think you're kidding us, Mr. Brandon. You'd never put

your good name at risk."

Stephen smiled. "I have entered the diplomatic field – and here my name *and* reputation is at risk!"

Again there was laughter, and as conversation became general, Julia went over to her brother. "You opened a pretty kettle of fish."

"Didn't I?" he agreed. "Your Mr. Brandon's quite a personality!"

"Don't believe everything he says."

"He wasn't joking, Julia, I could tell from the way he spoke." He glanced across at him. "He'd have made a wonderful pirate."

The words evoked a picture of Stephen as a swashbuckling mountebank. He certainly had the saturnine good looks and nerves of steel that the part required. But when Julia spoke her voice was prim.

"He would probably have died on the gallows!"

"Not Brandon. He's too cool a customer. I'd back him against anyone." Nick stifled a yawn, but not before Julia had seen it.

"Bed for you," she murmured, and led him upstairs to a small room opposite Stephen's suite.

"I didn't realise he was staying here," Nick said. "Bit hard on you having to live with two employers at the same time!"

"I don't regard Mrs. Rogers in that way," Julia said. "And Mr. Brandon's only here for a month."

Leaving Nick to settle down she returned to the living-room. Several of the guests had gone and Kim was talking to Stephen and May-lin, making it impossible for her not to join them.

"What's it like to have a hippy brother?" May-lin asked.

"That's an old-fashioned word these days," Julia replied.

"Each generation has its own hippies," Stephen interposed equably. "At Nick's age *I* also had a desire to reform the world."

"And now?" May-lin asked.

"Now I have enough of a problem reforming *myself*!"

Humour shifted the uneasy undercurrent and a few moments later Kim steered Julia to a settee.

"Every time I see you again you are more beautiful."

"And *your* compliments are just as flattering."

"It is not flattery." The softness of his voice was belied by the tautness of his slim body. "I am in love with you, Julia. You know that."

"Please – don't say any more."

"I must. This is not how I planned to tell you, but emotions cannot always be controlled." He stared into her face. "I want you to meet my parents."

Wishing she was a million miles away, she knew she had to face the reality of this difficult situation. A situation for which she had only herself to blame.

"I don't love you," she said gently. "I'm fond of you – very fond. But not enough for marriage."

"But you knew how I felt . . . I made it so clear." His voice was accusing. "And you continued to see me. You gave me every reason to hope." With an exclamation he stood up and pulled her to her feet. "We cannot talk here," he said, and led her out to the terrace.

"I didn't realise you wanted to marry me," she said, taking hold of the conversation before he could. "I knew you found me attractive, but I – "

"Don't lie!" His voice was sharp. "I made my intentions clear from the beginning. But we will not argue over the past. It is our future that concerns me. I want to marry you, Julia, to share my home and my life with you. And it will be a good life. I am going far; I promise you that."

"I'm sure you'll be extremely successful," she said gently, "but that doesn't affect my decision. I can't marry you, Kim. I don't love you."

"Is there anyone else?"

"No," she lied.

"Then I will make you change your mind. You were made for me. Fate sent you to Thailand."

"I don't believe in Karma," she answered lightly.

96

"I do," he said, "and my fate will be yours."

Pulling her into his arms, he kissed her with all the intensity she had expected. But it was impossible to lose herself in his desire, and though aware of his rasping breath and the tremble of his body, she remained totally passive in his arms. Her lack of response in no way disconcerted him, and when he drew back it was to look at her with speculative calm.

"You are frightened of me, Julia. That is why you don't respond. But as long as there is no one else, I will *make* you love me."

His confidence scared her, causing her to doubt her own strength of mind. Yet what he had said was ridiculous. He could not make her do anything. Besides, she *was* in love with someone else. For the first time her love for Stephen gave her comfort instead of pain.

"Let's go inside," she said. "I'm being bitten."

"By pangs of conscience, I hope!"

His wry humour restored her own, and they re-entered the living-room to find it deserted except for Mrs. Rogers, who was by the bureau looking at some photographs which Julia had taken.

Kim paused to admire them, then realising he was the last guest, reluctantly departed.

"Now I can go to bed," Mrs. Rogers sighed. "I thought I'd better stay around until he went. I recognised the light of love in his eyes!"

"Unrequited," Julia said dryly.

"You could do worse," Mrs. Rogers said thoughtfully.

"No. It's out of the question."

"Because you love Stephen?"

"Is it so obvious?"

"Only to me. But that's because I happen to be fond of you. I doubt if anyone else suspects."

"I hope you're right." Julia was grim. "I'd never want Stephen to guess."

"Are you sure he doesn't?"

"Positive. He likes me because he appreciates intelligence in women who work for him. But basically he despises women who have a career."

"You know the reason for that."

Julia drew a deep breath. "Sometimes I feel he hates *all* women. He needs them – he's very human in that way – but he hates himself for it."

"What a waste." Mrs. Rogers looked at Julia with pity. "You're so right for each other. That's why I tried to play matchmaker. If only I'd kept my mouth shut!"

"Don't worry about it," Julia said. "In a couple of weeks it will all be over."

The words echoed in her mind long after she had said them, as though reverberating down the lonely years that stretched ahead of her.

Soon it will all be over!

CHAPTER SEVEN

With Julia preoccupied with the conference, Nick accompanied Mrs. Rogers on her tours around Bangkok. He found her a knowledgeable guide and, for her part, she was amused by his irreverent comments and perceptive eye.

"If you could type," she said at Sunday lunch when he had been at the house a week, "I'd ask you to take Julia's place!"

"It's nice to know I'm needed," Julia grinned as she helped herself to salad.

They were eating beside the pool, both she and Nick in scanty swimsuits, shaded from the sun by a large coloured umbrella. It was the first time she had felt at ease since Stephen's arrival in Bangkok; knowing he was in the house had made her reluctant to wear her bikini except for an early morning swim before he left his room, or an occasional evening dip before he returned home. It was as though wearing clothes helped her to hide her feelings for him, or perhaps a fear that his eyes on her body would arouse her to a desire she would be unable to hide. But this week-end he was at May-lin's house at Pattaya Beach, and though his absence enabled her to relax, knowing with whom he was spending his time set her nerves on edge. Present or absent, the dratted man was always in her mind!

"I'm surprised May-lin didn't ask you both to join her," Mrs. Rogers said, divining where Julia's thought lay.

"Bitches don't share their bones," Nick chuckled.

"We've nothing in common," Julia said briskly. "Anyway, I wouldn't fancy playing gooseberry."

"Do you think Brandon will marry her?" Nick asked. "She doesn't look the sort who'd settle for anything else."

"Most women won't!" Mrs. Rogers informed him.

"*I* don't intend to get married," he said. "It's much more sensible to live together."

Julia and Mrs. Rogers smiled at one another and though he intercepted the look, Nick chose to ignore it and munched contentedly at a bowl of fresh vegetables: corn cobs only two inches long, radishes the size of baby tomatoes and carrots as sweet as sugarbeet.

"I'm going to miss all this," he said, waving his arm at the food, the swimming pool and the blue sky above. "I must leave here Wednesday at the latest."

"Are you hitching back?" Mrs. Rogers asked.

"No. Jakri's father bought me a return ticket – that was part of the arrangement – but I traded it in for one that would take me as far as Germany. I'll hitch from there."

"Why don't you fly *all* the way home?" Julia asked.

"Because I'd like to hitch through part of Europe, and I also got a bit of money back on the ticket. I want to buy a few things here," he added.

"You won't be able to load yourself up if you're hitching part of the way."

"I thought you could bring some things back for me."

"I knew you'd ask that!"

He laughed, and pushing back his chair, took a leaping dive into the pool.

Nick's high spirits made it difficult for Julia to mope, and though she occasionally remembered that Stephen and May-lin were together, she did not think of him in concrete terms until he returned home on Sunday evening.

He looked considerably more rested and a pang of jealousy went through her, but neither by look nor word did she give herself away, and when he asked if she would work with him for an hour, she immediately agreed.

With notebook in hand she felt closer to him than at any time, and mused bleakly that this was the nearest they would ever come to intimacy. He was still wearing the casual clothes he had travelled back in from Pattaya: beige slacks and open-necked shirt through which she glimpsed the tangle of dark hair on his chest. In the flower-filled sitting-room he exuded an over-powering aura of virility, and she forced herself to concentrate on her work, waiting for him to begin dictation. But for several moments he seemed lost in thought, and when he finally spoke it was to ask her how she thought the negotiations were going.

"I feel the General is under more pressure than he admits," she said.

"So do I. When we're alone together he sees every point before I can make it, but during the main meetings he pretends he doesn't understand me."

"He's arguing with you deliberately – trying to make certain members of his own delegation think he's putting up a fight."

Stephen raked long fingers through his hair. "I wish I knew if his opposition came from the left or the right faction."

"What difference would it make?"

"Know your enemy," he reminded her. "I hate fighting in the dark."

Abruptly he began to dictate, reading from notes he had made, and going so fast that she was hard put to keep up with him.

"I won't get all this typed back for the morning."

"I won't be needing it till noon. I'm lunching alone with the General." He stifled a yawn and stood up. "I'm hoping to settle all the main points with Sirit by tomorrow, but there are several things I'll have to talk over with the Committee in Brussels as well as the Prime Minister."

"Does that mean you'll have to fly home and come back?"

"Yes. I'll only be away a week – a fortnight at the most. I was hoping you'd come with me."

"I'm very happy with Mrs. Rogers," she said stiffly.

"I wasn't thinking in permanent terms. Only while the negotiations are going on. I'll need you as much in Brussels as I do here."

She looked at the floor, furious for having misunderstood him. "I'll have to ask Mrs. Rogers."

"I've already done so. She's quite agreeable."

Julia's head tilted sharply. "You take a lot for granted."

"Self-confidence is a necessary attribute for success!"

"I'd have called it conceit!"

His eyes glittered and she hurriedly stood up, holding her notebook in front of her like a shield. "I'll start the typing now," she said breathlessly.

"At this hour? Don't be crazy. Go and get some beauty sleep." The glitter increased. "Not that you need any. You're an extremely beautiful young woman." He sauntered to the door and held it open for her. "Goodnight."

When Julia came down next morning Stephen had already left the house, and she did not see him to speak to alone until they met at the Ministry a few moments before the afternoon meeting was due to begin.

"How did your luncheon go?" she whispered.

"It wasn't a business one. Sirit wants me to help a friend of his."

"I'm sorry, I didn't mean to pry. I hadn't realised it was personal."

"Neither had I." A faint smile curved his mouth, making the lower lip look unexpectedly sensual. "One of his aides has become involved with the 'minor wife' of a Minister and Sirit wants my help."

"Who for? The wife, the mistress or the lover?"

"Don't look so morally indignant!" he said amusedly. "Sirit only wants the aide out of the way for a few months. Any scandal now could do him a great deal of harm."

"Why? The General isn't responsible for the morals of his employees!"

"There are plenty of scandal sheets who'll say he encouraged the affair. A similar incident brought down the Government some years ago."

Remembering a scandal which had rocked England and nearly done the same, Julia appreciated the General's position.

"Can you help?" she asked.

"I'll find the man a job at the Bank."

The arrival of the General put an end to their conversation, and for the rest of the day Julia was too busy to give any more thought to it. The meeting was fraught with the usual arguments. The French and Belgian delegates not only disagreed with the Thais but also with each other, and Stephen expended a great deal of energy trying to placate his own party. But eventually he did so, though the strain was evident in the fine lines fanning out from his mouth.

It was late afternoon before the talks took a more progressive turn and, unwilling to stop, the delegates sustained themselves on coffee and cigars, making the air blue before they finally called it a day.

It was nine o'clock when Julia and Stephen returned home. Mrs. Rogers had taken Nick to see some Thai dancing, but the dining table had been set with a cold buffet which Stephen Brandon looked at with distaste.

"I can't face any food," he said, and moved jerkily across to the stairs.

With his hand on the banister he swayed, and without a word Julia ran over and propelled him to the living-room. Pushing him on to the settee, she placed a pillow behind his head. His skin had the pallor she had come to associate with a migraine attack and there were the familiar beads of sweat on his forehead.

"Where are your pills?"

"In my room."

She ran up to fetch them, painfully aware of the navy blue silk pyjamas folded in readiness for him on the bed, and his wine silk dressing gown draped across the arm of a chair. Quickly she ran downstairs again, gave him some pills and water and dimmed the lights.

"If there's anything you want I'll be in the next room."

He did not answer and she went into the dining-room. She was too tired to eat much, and after a snack tiptoed in to look at him. He was fast asleep, his breathing heavy, and she returned to the dining-room and placed some food on a tray, together with a thermos flask of coffee.

He still had his eyes closed when she went back to the living-room and she set the tray on the table. No man had the right to look so vulnerable when he was so much the opposite! She sat down and as she did so realised he was watching her.

"Have I been asleep long?"

"An hour. I've brought you some coffee and sandwiches."

"Excellent, I'm starving now." Gingerly he stood up, his movements growing assured as he found the pain had gone. "There must be something about you that brings on my migraine!" He yawned and stretched, then took one of the sandwiches offered.

"Perhaps you only work so hard when I'm around," she replied. "After all, no one else could keep up with your pace!"

"Actually you do spur me on," he smiled. "Like a young blood trying to prove himself!"

She reddened, but kept her composure. "What do you have to prove to me?"

"How successful I am. Isn't that what women admire in a man? Success and strength. The moment they find he has a weakness they use it to destroy him."

"You've a jaundiced view of women," she said.

"Maybe." He put his sandwich down half eaten, as though he found it tasteless, and she sensed that though he was putting things in terms of the present, his mind had gone back to the past, and that it was the lonely years of his youth and the bitterness of his father that he was remembering.

"You think it's wrong for a person to be entirely self-sufficient, don't you?" he murmured. "But it's the best way to live. Then no one can hurt you."

"You can't live alone. Not if you want a normal life."

"Mine's normal."

"Without love?"

"I have all the love I need."

"Sex!" There was a world of inflection in her voice and his eyebrows lifted sardonically. "Sex is the only reason a man ever gets married," he drawled.

"You can't believe that!"

"I do. Sex is the strongest force in the world."

"But not the *only* one."

"It is, where men and women are concerned."

"If your father brought you up to think like that, I'm not surprised *his* marriage failed!"

Stephen gave a strangled sound and fearfully Julia stopped, regretting her loss of control.

"You don't pull any punches, do you?" he commented in a surprisingly calm voice. "But I think I should make it clear that my feelings are my own. They have nothing to do with my father's attitude."

"But he brought you up," she said stubbornly. "He must have had some influence on the way you think."

"You're very persistent." He was not so calm now. "Are you suggesting he was wrong?"

"I'm suggesting you form your own judgement."

"About what?"

"Your mother."

"I have no wish to discuss my father's attitude to my mother," he said icily.

"But it's motivated your whole life. *Your* attitude to women has been coloured by everything your father taught you!"

"You know a lot about my private life."

She bit her lip, unwilling for him to know that Mrs. Rogers had talked to her about him. "I worked at your bank," she reminded him, "and people gossiped."

"So it seems. But like most gossip, it's wrong. My father loved my mother. Loved and worshipped her. When she left him, he was heartbroken. He did everything in his power to get her back."

"Everything except let her lead the life she'd been trained for!"

"Trained for?" he exclaimed. "What about the obligation of marriage?"

"Marriage is a *part* of one's life. Not the whole of it. Your mother didn't expect your father to give up *his* work and devote all his time to *her*?"

"Don't be ridiculous!"

"It's no more ridiculous than what your father wanted. Your mother was a successful biologist when she married him. Why should he have expected her to give it all up?"

"It's a wife's duty to – "

"Love her husband and family," Julia interrupted. "But that doesn't mean giving up her own life! If your father wanted that kind of a woman he should have chosen someone else."

"Perhaps my mother shouldn't have married in the first place," Stephen Brandon said furiously. "She certainly shouldn't have had a child! Or do you think it normal to desert your husband and baby in favour of a test tube in Brazil?"

"*Did* she desert you?" Julia questioned.

"What's that supposed to mean?"

"I thought your mother took you with her when she travelled?"

"Only till I was six."

"Six is a long time. Why do you talk as if she deserted you in the cradle!"

"It felt like it," he burst out.

"Only because your father wanted you to think so! He must have made you feel so guilty about loving your mother that you tried to pretend you were never with her! That's why you speak as if the first six years of your life didn't count."

"You're jumping to fantastic conclusions."

"Are they fantastic? I'm going on the things you say . . . what you do . . . your whole attitude to women." She flung out her hands. "You think it's wrong for a woman to want marriage *and* a career. That's why you spend your time with dumb beauties and run a mile from anyone with a brain! If you haven't the sense to realise that such an attitude went out with the dodo, then your father didn't just indoctrinate you – he must have brainwashed you as well!"

Stephen's eyes glittered with temper. "If you think that, why waste time on me?"

"I don't think it," she said crossly. "At least I do, but I think there's hope for you! I know I'm putting my head in a noose, but I can't help it. Doesn't it strike you as odd that you should have tried to forget the years you shared with your mother? Don't you think it shows how guilty you felt about loving her?"

"Guilty? You must be joking!"

"I'm not. You felt that loving your mother was being disloyal to your father. That's why you've tried to blank out the years you spent with her. Why you go on insisting that your ideal woman is someone who has no life apart from her home and family. If you could let yourself think clearly you'd know I was speaking the truth. But you're determined to follow what your father taught you – to prove you're a loving son."

"Since he's been dead for — "

"His memory isn't," she interrupted

"That's true," came the quiet reply. "I often remember how unhappy he was. You shouldn't be surprised that I blame my mother for it."

"Why blame either of them? Why not accept the fact that they were wrong for each other?"

"It isn't so easy to forget your past."

"At least try not to make it so hard!"

"I suppose you want me to believe I had a wonderful mother," he said sarcastically.

"Wasn't she? I heard she was brilliant in her own field. And she obviously loved you. If she hadn't, she wouldn't have wanted you with her. You can't blame her because your father took you away."

"He wanted me too."

"That was part of the problem," Julia agreed. "They both wanted you. But why blame your mother more?"

"Because she was the one to leave home."

"She had a brain and she was impelled to use it. Your father knew that when he married her. If he had tried to understand her – to meet her half-way. . . ."

"By giving up his own career and following her?"

"Perhaps they could have worked out a compromise." She took a deep breath. "I'd just like you to see that your mother wasn't completely in the wrong."

"Would that make me fall in love with a brainy woman?" he countered. "Why not accept the fact that I prefer dumb ones who make no demands on me?"

"If you do, then I've wasted my time," she said with an effort at lightness. "I'm sorry."

"You're not sorry at all! There's still the light of battle in your eyes!"

She stared at him, surprised. Expecting his anger, she found his amusement disconcerting.

"You haven't agreed with one single thing I've said," she accused.

"At least I have listened. So count yourself lucky."

"Oh, I do. After all, you could have fired me!" She stood up. "From now on you can waste your life – if that's what you want."

She moved to the door, but he was ahead of her, barring the way.

"Why not accept me the way I am?" he asked softly.

"It isn't my duty to accept you at all," she said in careful tones. "Besides, I'm the sort of girl you don't like – I love my work and I'm hoping to make a career for myself in photography!"

"I'm willing to overlook that!" Before she could guess his

intention he pulled her into his arms. "How obstinate you are. It must be the red in that wine-coloured hair of yours!"

She tried to pull away from him, but her movement only made him grasp her more firmly. His eyes stared into hers, and as she stared back their colour seemed to intensify. Or was she seeing her own reflection in them?

"There must be some way of shutting you up," he said huskily, and covered her mouth with his own.

It was the first real physical contact they had ever had, and though Julia had dreamed of this moment, the reality of it was a blow to her pride. She had derided him for finding comfort in the easiest possible way, and he was showing her just how easy it was!

Angrily she fought him, arching her back to push him away. But his grip tightened and his body pressed hard against hers, while all the while his mouth was like fire on her own, seeking an answering passion she longed to give and desperately tried not to.

Aware of her resistance, he seemed determined to make her capitulate, and the pressure of his mouth grew more gentle, momentarily disarming her. But even as her errant body cried out for his, her mind took over, and with a strength that surprised her she pushed him away.

"Leave me alone," she cried. "You've no right to take advantage of me!"

"That's the last thing in the world I want to do." There was an unfathomable look in his eyes. "You are one of the few women I can trust."

"Despite what I said?"

"Perhaps because of it. At least you see me as a person in my own right – not just a rich meal-ticket!"

"You get what you deserve," she retorted.

He laughed. "Still sharpening your tongue on me?"

"I'm sorry, I didn't mean to."

"Show me *how* sorry you are," he said, and once more drew her close.

This time she did not resist him. Instead her arms came round his neck, drawing him close as if he were the little boy of her imagination. Their lips met again, and there was no desire for mastery in his touch; only an urgent passion that communicated itself to her.

Time lost its meaning and so did identity. They were male and female seeking completeness in one another; trying to assuage passion in total union.

But such a union had to be denied, and even as Julia longed to give what Stephen was demanding, some part of her held back. This was not the kind of love she had dreamed of; it was better to be unfulfilled than to give in now and hate herself for the rest of her life.

"I can't!" she cried. "It isn't right!"

"It seems very right to me!" There was a faint smile on his mouth. "You are an extremely beautiful young woman."

His tone, more than his words, roused her to anger. "Propinquity," she reminded him. "Like the man who married his secretary!"

Stephen drew back. "The one thing that spoils the female sex," he drawled, "is their habit of total recall! If propinquity had anything to do with my kissing you, I would have done so weeks ago, months ago even. I had plenty of opportunity in London."

"I looked different then."

He stared at her, puzzled. Then his brow cleared. "The way you look isn't important. It's the way you talk and think that matters – and that's always been the same. Even now when I think of you I remember the way you *used* to look. I've told you that before."

"I know, but I find it hard to believe."

"It's true," he persisted.

Unsure what to say, she took the safe way out. "It's been a

long day and I'm tired. I'm going to bed."

Her hand was on the door when his own came out to cover it, dark and strong on her slender one. "I really am sorry, Julia. I hope this won't affect your working with me?"

She suppressed a shiver. How concerned he was that loss of control lose might him a capable secretary! With an immense effort she forced herself to look at him. "Why should it? Even the most controlled people forget themselves!"

"I didn't forget," he said roughly, "I remembered."

"Remembered what?"

"Your sweetness . . . your understanding."

She longed to take the words at face value but knew it would be dangerous to do so. "I try my best to please," she said lightly.

Devilment glinted in his eyes. "Does that mean I can take it as part of a regular service?"

"I'm only your temporary – remember?"

His laugh was real, and she hurried out before he could reply. But memory of his kiss lay inside her like a nugget of gold to be taken out, examined with care and hidden away again before it disappeared. It was all she would have to remember him by, for she must never let it happen again.

Her sleep that night was restless, and at seven o'clock she jumped out of bed, put on her swim-suit and padded down to the pool. For half an hour she swam, then, pleasantly tired, she floated, enjoying the buoyancy of the water and the warmth of the sun on her face.

"You're up early, Julia."

A drawling voice startled her and she gasped, spluttered and sank to the bottom, coming to the surface choking and shaking her head.

"Mr. Brandon!" she coughed out some water, "I didn't see you."

Strong arms reached over and pulled her out of the pool. "It wasn't my intention to drown you! I didn't know my presence would give you such a shock."

She reached for her towelling coat and dived into it, aware of how little her bikini hid. Stephen was overcome by no such inhibition, and in brief black swimming trunks settled casually in a chair.

"Do you think you could possibly stop calling me Mr. Brandon? We've gone too far for that."

"It was knowing how far I went that gave me a sleepless night," she said candidly. "I want to apologise again."

"Forget it." He stretched his long legs in front of him and the muscles of his thighs rippled beneath his bronzed skin. "Actually I didn't sleep much either. I kept thinking of what you said. You put up a good argument, Julia. You would have made a good psychologist."

"I'd have made a bad one I'm afraid. I would get too involved."

"Yet you advocate involvement for me."

"We're talking about different things. Involvement in one's career is different from involvement in one's personal life."

"But my life *is* my career."

"More's the pity!" She stood up and belted her towelling coat more tightly around her.

"I won't need you this morning," he said, "so you're free to go out with your brother. I feel guilty at not being able to let you spend more time with him."

"I'm happy just having him around. If you're giving me the time off because of that . . ."

"I'm not," he said shortly. "If I needed you, I'd use you."

"Yes, Mr. Brandon."

"And don't call me Mr. Brandon!"

"It's force of habit."

"Then force yourself out of it! It wasn't difficult for *me*."

"I haven't got your strength of mind," she said sweetly, and heard his laugh mocking her as she ran across the lawn to the house.

CHAPTER EIGHT

With the morning free to do as she wished Julia went in search of Nick, only to be told with brotherly candour that he intended to spend the day sunbathing.

"If that's the case, I'll go out and take some photographs," she replied. "I'll be back for lunch."

Protected from the glare by sun-hat and dark glasses, Julia snapped her way through the Chinese quarter of the city, an area whose bustle and intensity was at variance with the rest of Bangkok. No wonder it was said that the Chinese ruled the industry and allowed the Thais to rule the country! Tiny one-roomed shops – open to the street – were packed full of wares, no matter whether it was sacks of rice, bales of shimmering silk or the enormous variety of shiny tin dishes used as cooking utensils and decoration.

The pavements themselves were crowded with stalls, their owners clutching at passers-by, cajoling them to stop and lowering their price with every moment of hesitation until, sensing a change in mood, they reached a figure at which a sale could be made.

Noon found Julia by the Suan Pakkad Palace, and seeing visitors entering it she took the opportunity of following them. For an hour she wandered spellbound among the rare antiques that filled the interior; they comprised almost every branch of Thai art, from carved ivory and glass mosaic to inlaid mother of pearl on hand-carved teak.

The garden around the Palace was exquisite, and in it stood a seventeenth-century lacquer pavilion, furnished with gold and lacquer chests on which were painted scenes of Hell that reminded her of some of the more grotesque works of Hieronymus Bosch. The main difference was that Hanuman, the Monkey

God, was seen everywhere: peeping out from intricately painted foliage and visible between the detailed miniatures of rabbits and peacocks and snakes.

The arrival of some twenty American tourists sent her back into the street again and, tired by the heat and her sleepless night, she decided to return home and rest. If she didn't, she might fall asleep this afternoon when working for Stephen!

Stephen! She said his name aloud, savouring the word as though it were the man himself. Again she remembered the way he had kissed her: not the first hard bruising kiss but the second tender one, when she had clung to him and nearly given herself away.

The insistent blare of a hooter jerked her round to stare at a white sports car. May-lin was at the wheel, her black hair glistening in the sunlight, her expression masked by dark glasses.

"Julia!" she called. "I thought it was you." Disregarding the traffic hooting behind her, the girl swung her car into the curb. "If you're going back to Mrs. Rogers', I'll give you a lift."

It was impossible to refuse the offer and Julia slid into the front seat, holding her breath as they shot out into the mainstream of traffic.

For a while they drove in silence. Despite her air of fragility May-lin was an expert driver. Expert according to Thai standards, Julia amended, as with bland disregard for a single-decker bus, they swung directly in its path and turned sharp left, making the vehicle behind them brake protestingly.

"You're still busy taking photographs," May-lin commented.

"There's so much to record," Julia smiled. "I don't think I'll ever finish!"

"You looked very professional – all those lenses and things!"

"It was a present from Stephen."

The car quickened speed, almost as though it had given a spurt of anger. But May-lin's voice was casual when she spoke again. "Do you mind helping him? Once you've left someone, isn't it embarrassing to work for them again?"

"Only if you've left them because of a quarrel. And I had no argument with Stephen," Julia lied. "I left because I wanted to travel."

"Do you regret the change?"

"Not at all. Being here is like living in a different world."

"It's made you look different too." Again the car spurted forward and slowed down. "The change in your appearance is remarkable. What caused it?"

Julia knew it would be silly to pretend she did not understand the question, and pointless to lie about the answer.

"Stephen had always employed a particular type of woman," she said carefully, "and when I applied for the job I – I decided the only way to get it was to act the part."

"You're a girl of obvious resources. You should go far!"

"I've come to Thailand!"

"That wasn't what I meant." There was a pause. "I'm glad you're working with Stephen while he's here. He needs someone he can rely on."

Julia knew the words had been said deliberately to put her in her place and she tried not to let them irritate her.

"*I* try to make him take things easy," May-lin continued, "but he seems to enjoy pushing himself."

"He works best when he's pushed for time," Julia said candidly. "The only trouble is that it gives him migraine."

May-lin nodded. "He had an attack during the week-end. It was frightening to watch." The car made another left turn. "It woke me up in the middle of the night. His breathing had altered completely. I was so frightened I didn't know what to do." The silk-clad shoulders lifted expressively. "Luckily he had his pills with him and I gave him one."

Julia stared sightlessly through the window. She now knew why May-lin had offered her a lift back to the house: to let her know her relationship with Stephen. Not that it needed to be put into words. In this day and age Stephen was unlikely to have remained on platonic terms with the girl. Yet coming from the arms of such a beautiful creature, how quickly he had been roused to passion by another; thus invalidating both emotions.

"Would you like to live in Thailand permanently?" May-lin was speaking again, "or would you find it too strange?"

"It's the strangeness that I love," With an effort Julia forced herself to concentrate on the question. The whole philosophy – the way of life here – is so much more peaceful than anything I've known – apart from the traffic!" she added. "That's the worst!"

Dexterously May-lin swerved to avoid an oncoming car. "Most drivers only sit on half their seats so that Buddha can sit next to them!" she said lightly. "They don't worry about getting killed because they know they'll be reborn."

"That's fine if you're a Buddhist," Julia retorted, "but I'm not!"

"It's a satisfying religion. If one believes in rebirth one is not frightened of death."

"Faith can't be forced," Julia responded.

"It would come naturally if you married a Thai."

"I'm hardly likely to do that."

"Really? I thought you and Kim . . ."

The soft voice lingered on an upraised note, but Julia refrained from replying, glad to see Mrs. Rogers' driveway ahead.

"I'm supposed to be lunching here with Stephen," May-lin said. "I hope he won't be late."

"I can see him." Julia pointed to the tall figure sauntering across the grass towards them. Before he could reach the car she was half-way up the steps to the house, and heard his voice behind her, low and warm as he greeted the Thai girl.

Tears blurred Julia's vision and she crossed the hall, not seeing Nick until she bumped into him. He grinned and steadied her and, forcing an answering grin to her face, she looked at the packages he was carrying.

"Don't tell me my clever young brother's fallen for tourist junk!"

"Things are so cheap here," he said sheepishly, "it would have been crazy not to buy them."

"What sort of things?"

"Worry beads and pipes and Buddhas. I can sell them for ten times the price in England."

"You'll pay ten times the price to fly them home!"

"I thought you'd take some for me. You're only coming back for a week, so you won't need much luggage."

Conceding the point, Julia took some of the parcels from him, and as she moved to the stairs was aware of Stephen and May-lin watching her.

"Not *yours*?" Stephen's black brows raised as he took in her assorted packages.

"Mine," Nick answered, "but Julia's taking them back for me."

"Sisters have their uses," May-lin laughed, and put her hand possessively on Stephen's arm.

Quickly Julia mounted the stairs, her heart throbbing so loudly that it obliterated all other sounds.

Unwilling to see May-lin and Stephen together, she had a fruit lunch in her room, and did not go downstairs until Stephen sent a maid to call her.

"I told you I wanted you this afternoon," he said irritably as she reached the hall.

"I didn't realise you were waiting for me."

"May-lin left immediately after lunch," he said, and strode out to the car, pausing impatiently for her to climb in.

Aware of his nearness, she became aware of every nerve in her own body, yet she gave no sign of the turmoil within her as she racked her brains for something to say. No words came to mind and the memory of how she had responded to him last night was overlaid by memory of what May-lin had said. Had Stephen fallen asleep against that slender body, clasped in those pale, twining arms? The thought made her tremble and Stephen touched her arm lightly.

"Don't be upset about it, Julia."

Shock coursed through her and she flung him a startled look.

"You make it so obvious," he went on.

She struggled for something to say, but no words came.

"Nick isn't a child," Stephen continued, "he'll be perfectly all right hitchhiking from Germany. Far safer than his journey to get here!"

Julia's relief that Stephen had misunderstood the reason for her agitation was so great that it reverberated in her voice, giving it such an emotional overtone that he did not believe her when she said she wasn't worrying about her brother at all.

"Of course you are. I can see it in your eyes when you look at him. Your trouble is that you have a strong protective urge."

"Only to those I love," she said, and hastily added: "And those I feel sorry for."

"I obviously come into the second category!"

Silence hung in the air as heavy as a curtain, and feeling it weigh on them she tried to shift it.

"If you've been responsible for someone for a long time it's hard to stop – even though you know there's no more need for it. I keep telling myself Nick's grown up – that in some respects he's even more adult than I am – but I still feel I have to protect him!"

"What women see as protection is usually smothering!"

"We'd better keep off that subject! You remember where it led last night."

Too late she realised what she had said, and though she kept her eyes averted, she felt his sharp look. But when he spoke it was to talk about something quite different.

"I know you want to stay with Mrs. Rogers until she's finished her book, but how do you feel about returning to the Bank afterwards?"

"It's never good to go back."

"Don't be trite! Think about it, Julia. I work better with you than with anyone else. You understand me . . . I don't need to explain things to you . . . Think it over," he repeated.

The desire to do as he asked was so strong that only by being vehemently negative could she fight it. "No, Stephen. It wouldn't work. I'll never return to you."

Only as she saw the hardness on his face did she realise how much her emphatic refusal had angered him, for with a curt shrug he lowered his head and studied the papers in his hand.

She searched for a way to apologise, but every sentence that came to mind seemed as though it would give her feelings away, and she decided it was safer to let him think what he liked.

For the rest of the week she was too busy to think of herself. With Christmas approaching, Stephen took a firmer hand on the negotiations, for the European delegates were resentful at not being home with their families, though everyone pretended they were too sophisticated to care.

With her usual supreme confidence Mrs. Rogers decided to give a traditional Christmas dinner and, with this organised, decided she would also decorate the house. Both Nick and Julia elected to do this job, and for several days happily pinned and tacked and hammered.

Only Stephen remained aloof from it all, surveying with a jaundiced eye the festive arrangements going on around him.

"I'd abolish Christmas if I could," he said a few days before Christmas Eve. "It's the worst thing in the world for families to get together. It always leads to rows. Analysts say their couches are crowded for three months afterwards!"

"What a Mrs. Grundy you are!" Absorbed in decorating an artificial Christmas tree, Julia did not monitor her words. It was the first time for days that she had spoken to him in such a teasing manner, and momentarily he was taken aback, the look on his face giving him away.

"I'm sorry you feel like that about Christmas," she apologised quietly. "I suppose these decorations *are* silly when there aren't any children around to enjoy them."

"*You're* a child," he drawled. "You're doing it for yourself."

His comment came into her mind when she went to buy him a present and after only a slight hesitation she chose a gilt paperweight carved into the likeness of the three wise monkeys with eyes, ears and mouth covered. Only as she wrapped it up did she wonder if he might read more into it than she had meant. Or had she subconsciously wanted to provoke him again? Either way it was too late to buy him anything else, and she left his gift nestling among the other packages at the foot of the tree in the hall before going to bed on Christmas Eve.

Knowing that to keep open house during the holidays would invite a deluge of visitors, Mrs. Rogers had decided to make it a family-only affair, though this included May-lin and Kim. Kim had been invited despite Julia's protestations that to continue seeing him when she had refused to marry him was heartless. But he had persuaded Mrs. Rogers to ignore this and had dismissed Julia's feeling of guilt by making it clear he did not consider her answer as final! In normal circumstances she would have insisted that they did not meet again, but with Stephen in the house she decided to utilise Kim's presence both as emotional support and camouflage.

Christmas Day dawned sunny, with a deep blue sky and palm trees rustling in a cool breeze. Memory of other Christmases reminded Julia of the happy days when her parents had been alive, and her first few waking hours were tinged with sadness. But at midday when they all gathered in the hall to open their Christmas presents there was no room for anything except pleasure, and she exclaimed with delight at the gold necklace and earrings Mrs. Rogers had bought her, while Nick's fleecy slippers provoked wild laughter. May-lin's gift was a set of anonymous toiletries and Kim's an outsize flagon of scent which made her realise that though he said he loved her, he did not understand her.

Stephen's present took her by surprise, and staring at the lapis lazuli locket nestling in its black velvet box she wished she could have opened it without prying eyes watching her. As she held the fine chain between her fingers she was aware that Stephen had come to kneel beside her.

"Do you like it, Julia?"

"It's exquisite. When did you find time to get it?"

"I bought it in England."

Taken aback, she sat on her heels and stared at him. "But I . . . but how did you know you'd meet me here?"

"You were in Bangkok and I had every intention of seeing you."

Remembering how plain and dowdy she had looked when working for him in England, she could not help wondering why. "Do you always treat your ex-secretaries so generously?"

"Only when they have an irritating habit of remaining in my thoughts!" He touched the stone with his finger. "I'd like to see you wear it."

She put it around her neck, but her fingers fumbled with the clasp and he reached out to help her, his hands resting for a moment on the nape of her neck.

Slowly she turned to face him and his eyes rested on the deep blue stone lying between the curve of her breasts.

"Your throat is made for diamonds," he said softly. "Kim would give them to you if you said the word."

"I don't need diamonds that much!"

"I hope you'll always feel the same. Never marry for expediency."

Their eyes met, and behind his a spark flickered, burned for an instant and then died.

"I must look at *my* present," he said in conversational tones, and quickly unwrapped the paper. As he saw the three wise monkeys his mouth quirked and the look he shot her was compounded of amusement and irritation.

"You can't resist a moral even when buying me a present!

Do these monkeys depict me as I am or as you'd like me to be?"

"It's a paperweight," she protested, "not a comment on your character!"

"I don't believe you." His smile deepened. "At least you didn't buy me a copy of the famous Rodin?"

"Why should I have?"

"His statue – the one called 'The Kiss'. It would have been appropriate, don't you think?"

Unable to think of a biting retort, she got to her feet and went back to the centre of the room.

For the remainder of the day she was able to avoid talking to him alone, though her feeling of relief was tinged with jealousy when he left in the afternoon to spend the rest of the day and the next at May-lin's house in Pattaya.

Though able to close her mind to Stephen's present relationship with the Thai girl, she could not help wondering if he planned a future with her. He had been determined not to pursue May-lin when she had left England, but the fact that fate had brought him to Thailand might make him decide she had a place in his life after all. She was lovely enough to make any man lose his senses, and since she appeared to demand little from him except admiration she might well be the sort of wife he wanted.

Yet try as she would, Julia was unable to forget the many glimpses he had given her of the lonely man who lay beneath the façade he showed to the world. Such a man needed companionship; a marriage of mind as well as body. But unless he could stop running away from his past he would never accept this fact, and with all her heart Julia wished she could make him realise this. Even though she would never share his future, it hurt her to think what he was allowing his future to become.

CHAPTER NINE

THE following evening, determined not to be home when Stephen returned from Pattaya, Julia went with Nick to the Rajadamnoen Stadium to watch a display of Thai-style boxing.

It was the national sport and the panoply with which the rival boxers presented themselves in the ring was fascinating. Clad in flashy silken robes, each man moved down the aisle to his corner where, before entering the ring, he knelt and prayed. Then with robes removed but head covered with a strand of rope – a sacred headband – he entered the ring to the wild applause of his supporters, and performed the traditional ritual of obeisance to the guardian spirit of his trainer and teacher. Depending on where he had trained was the ritual he performed. Some were like ballets in their grace and movement, while others were acrobatic. But once these rites were completed and the contest began, violence superseded everything else.

No part of the boxer's body was out of bounds to his opponent, and elbows, knees and feet as well as fists were used. Muscular arms and legs aimed punches everywhere, and as feet hardened by massage and exercise came into contact with chin, stomach or groin, there were loud cries of pain. Soon both men were streaming with sweat and blood, and the four-piece orchestra which played suitable accompaniment to the match began a more frenzied tune, whipping the packed stadium into a screaming mass of blood-hungry avengers.

Nausea overcame Julia's admiration for the courage of the boxers, and she was glad when the bell sent them back to their corners to rest. It was incredible that the gentle Thais had such a fierce national sport, for though she appreciated the skill involved she was far more aware of the violence. It epitomised something she had sensed but not fully comprehended in the Thai character: a power beneath the gentleness, an iron determination beneath the charm.

Not until she had come to the Stadium had she appreciated the difference between Western and Eastern culture. Part of the crowd, yet apart from it, she felt completely alien, and wondered if Kim experienced the same feeling when he watched a cricket match in England or a baseball match in America. He seemed so Westernised it was difficult to believe he did. Perhaps if she lived in Thailand long enough she too would grow accustomed to the fierce sport she had just seen.

At the end of the evening she was exhausted: partly from exhilaration at watching such a display of courage and partly from fear that such courage might result in serious injury. No wonder Kim had once told her a fighter rarely continued for more than five years. It was doubtful if any Western-style boxer – faced with a Thai opponent – would be able to continue for five weeks!

"What a strange mixture the Thais are." Nick echoed Julia's feelings as they strolled in the direction of home, deciding to walk for a while before flagging down a taxi. "After tonight, I don't think I understand them at all."

"I know exactly what you mean."

"Do you think you could marry a Thai?" he asked suddenly.

"Do you mean Kim?"

He gave an embarrassed grunt. "I don't mean to pry."

"You're not; you've a right to know." They walked a bit further. "I've no intention of marrying Kim," she said at last. "I don't love him."

"That's a relief. I'd miss you if you lived here the whole time."

"I'll be back by the time you leave Cambridge."

"I don't need to live *with* you," he said hastily. "Just as long as I know you're around!"

It was an admission that filled her with pleasure and she

squeezed his arm, the nearest she could come to affection without embarrassing him.

Two day later Nick left for home, but Julia was too inundated with work to have a chance to be depressed. The conference had already achieved a high degree of success and though there were still several areas of disagreement, Stephen was convinced these could be overcome.

"If the General could make the decision himself," she heard Stephen say to one of his own party, "he'd have agreed to everything by now. But he has a strong left-wing faction to contend with."

Almost as though he had appeared on cue the General came down the corridor, and Stephen walked forward to meet him. As always the two men greeted each other punctiliously, careful not to display the friendliness they did when they were alone together.

"I am sorry to have kept you waiting, Stephen," the General said. "*You* only have the conference to worry about, but I have many other things to do."

"We are always prepared to wait," Stephen said politely.

"No, no, I don't want to cause a delay. The sooner you can return home to make your report, the sooner you will be back to finalise it." He sighed. "And I want the agreement ratified as quickly as possible."

"Are there problems?" Stephen spoke so quietly that only Julia, standing to one side of him, could hear.

"In this country there are always problems!" the General murmured. "New wings like to be used and it is dangerous to try and clip them. But let us talk of more pleasant things. I have arranged a party for the Delegation for the day after tomorrow. I hope that will suit you?"

"But of course."

White teeth flashed in a dark face. "Spoken like a true diplomat, Stephen!"

Laughing, the two men went into the conference room, Julia and her Belgian counterpart bringing up the rear.

At the end of the meeting the General came over and spoke to the secretaries, bestowing words of praise on both of them, though he spoke slightly longer to Julia.

"I understand you wokred for Stephen Brandon in England," he said. "He told me you left him because you wished to travel."

"But I'm still working for him!" she smiled.

"Because he travelled too!" She laughed and he looked at her appreciatively. "I hope I will have the pleasure of seeing you at my party?"

"I didn't realise the secretaries were being invited."

"But naturally. No cog is so small that it is unimportant in a wheel!"

It was an apt turn of phrase, and Julia was still amused by it two nights later when she stood in the glittering ballroom of the Siam Intercontinental Hotel and watched the dancers on the floor. Determined to avoid the usual formality of a ministerial party, the General had made the venue the most sophisticated hotel in Bangkok.

Kim, as a junior aide, was forced to circulate among all the women, for which Julia was heartily relieved, though she was careful not to show it. Thank goodness she would be returning to England for a week. When she came back she would make a point of not seeing him so frequently. It was the only way to stop him from being hopeful. Even as she thought this she saw him bearing down on her and, stepping behind a potted palm tree, she slipped out on to the terrace.

The grounds of the hotel were extensive and she had the impression of walking in a park. The large extension loomed up high on her left, but the main part of the hotel – which housed the reception hall, dining-rooms and shops – was single-storied and topped by a giant, pagoda-shaped roof. From this main building snaked several double-storied ones which housed the more expensive suites, their windows overlooking the illuminated trees and shrubs.

Idly she wandered down one path and then another, swinging the Nikon camera which had caused comment from Mrs. Rogers when she had left the house with it earlier that evening.

"I don't think we need pictures of the General's party for my book, Julia dear!"

"If I manage to take any pictures they'll be for *me*," Julia grinned. "I'd like to get some shots of some of the delegates."

"We'll make a roving reporter of you yet! I'm sure you could sell some photographs to the British papers."

"Stephen would never forgive me if I did."

She remembered this conversation as she continued her stroll. So far to-night she had only used up half a roll of film, and she decided to place the camera in the cloakroom with her coat. Turning to go back to the hotel she was struck by the beauty of the huge roof whose thin spire seemed to pierce the blackness of the sky. As she paused to look at it the clouds moved away from the face of the moon, and silver light bathed the edges of the trees and lay across the water of the swimming pool like a platinum bar.

On the far side of the pool a man and woman moved and Julia drew back sharply, unwilling to intrude on a love scene. But the couple did not move close together and although they were too far away to hear what they were saying, there was a tenseness about them that made her feel she was witnessing something secret. Thoughts of sabotage raced through her brain, but even as it acted on her pulse, the breeze stirred the leaves and, through a moving branch, a moonbeam touched the dark head of the woman, illuminating her features. It was May-lin.

Instantly Julia's fear vanished and she smiled at her foolishness. In the tree directly above her head an animal stirred and she stepped back hastily. From this angle she had a different view of the hotel, the edge of the building jutting out in geometric precision against the skyline, the area to the left of it zig-zagged by the spiky fronds of a palm. It was such an unusual combination of lines and curves that she was reminded of an abstract painting, and automatically she brought the camera lens to her eye and clicked the shutter. As she did so the man beside May-lin handed her a package, its shiny cover reflecting the moonlight so vividly that it seemed to trap the moon itself. Irritated by the unexpected movement of the couple, which might have caused her to shake and blur her photograph, she took another shot of the scene, then, reluctant to let May-lin know she was there, she moved back into the shrubbery and made her way round to the main entrance.

The air-conditioning struck cold against her bare shoulders, and quickly leaving her camera in the cloakroom she returned to the warmth of the ballroom. After the black and silver of the night it seemed a blaze of colour, the khaki uniforms of the military highlighting the vivid silks of long dresses and the white dinner jackets of the European men.

"May I?" a deep voice asked, and she looked round and saw Stephen.

Silently she followed him on to the dance floor. Simultaneously the overhead lights lowered and the fast tempo of a samba gave way to a slow, pulsating rhythm that echoed the beat of her heart.

"You're the only woman here wearing black," he said. "You should wear it more often."

"Because it keeps me in the background?"

"Because it highlights your colouring. With skin and hair like yours, you're colourful enough."

"Thank you, sir," she replied.

His grip tightened. "I mean it. Black makes your skin glow like a pearl."

She missed a step and was angry that embarrassment had made her do so. To hide it she was flippant again. "Artificial or cultured?"

"Neither! You're *real*. Though right now you're acting artificial! What's wrong, Julia, does dancing with me make you nervous?"

"Petrified," she retorted, seeing the truth as the best way of lying. "After watching you dance with all these beautiful Thai women, I must feel like an Amazon to you."

He chuckled. "You still seem little. I suppose it's because you're graceful."

She missed a step and he gave her a shake. "Tired of dancing with me?"

"Just tired."

"I've been working you too hard. When we return from England you must have a holiday."

Her surge of pleasure at his words ebbed as he went on: "You can stay at May-lin's house at Pattaya. The bathing there is marvellous."

"It's generous of you to offer me someone else's hospitality!"

"May-lin won't mind. She won't be there anyway. She's leaving Thailand in a month."

Though she had been expecting this, hearing the words gave her a shock that robbed her cheeks of colour.

"You *are* tired," Stephen said, noticing her pallor, and drew her off the floor and into an alcove sheltered from sight by an enormous basket of pink, scentless roses.

"They're like beautiful women," he murmured. "Lovely to look at but lacking the essential essence!"

"I thought you only needed beauty." Shakily she sat down and, no longer needing strength to support herself, used the strength to control her manner.

"What makes *you* a judge of what I need?" he asked. She did not answer and he leaned closer. "If I made as many guesses about what *you* think as you do about what *I* think, we'd come to blows!"

She could not help smiling, "I bet I've been your most intractable secretary. You must have been pleased to get rid of me."

"You know that isn't true. I've already asked you to come back. I'm not repeating the offer," he added hastily. "I don't want my head snapped off again!"

"I'd like to apologise about that." She forced herself to look directly at him. "I was unnecessarily rude. I didn't mean it."

"Does that mean you might change your mind?"

"No. It – it wouldn't work."

"It's worked out here."

"Because the atmosphere's different. You're living at Mrs. Rogers' house. In London you would revert to normal and – " she hesitated, then decided to tell him part of the truth. "I might resent you acting the complete employer again."

"I see." He gave a sigh. "Seeing it from that point of view, you're probably right."

Disappointment flooded through her. If he had denied what she had said she would have been angry with him, yet his acceptance of it made her realise how far apart they already were. Clutching at her pride, she stood up.

"I think I'll go home. I feel exhausted."

"You look it."

"That must mean I look a sight!"

"It means you look vulnerable." There was a seriousness about him that made her realise he meant what he said, and the retort she had intended to make died on her lips.

"I sometimes get the impression you're putting on an act with me, Julia. I feel I'm not seeing the real you at all. That's why, when you're like this – tired and not fighting me any more – I feel I'm seeing the part of you that counts."

Feeling she was treading on water, she said carefully: "Most of us wear a mask from time to time. You're a dynamic and demanding person, Stephen. The only way to cope with you is to put up a defence."

She moved away from him and he followed her as she went to collect her jacket and camera.

"Use my car and chauffeur," he said. "I don't want you to go in a taxi at night."

He propelled her towards the British Embassy car that had been assigned to him and told the driver to take her home, waiting until she was in the back seat before he murmured "Good night" and returned to the hotel.

Tears blurred him from sight and she was glad he was too far away to see them, though even if he had he would have assumed they were from fatigue. She *was* tired, she admitted, sniffing miserably into her handkerchief; tired of fighting her love for him, of pretending she would be able to forget him. As if distance could dim his memory!

Misery washed over her anew and, regardless of the chauffeur's impassive back, she buried her head in her hands and burst into tears.

CHAPTER TEN

WITH one more day before their return to England there was crisis after crisis. Confidential minutes were lost and finally retrieved from a young attaché's briefcase; a junior Thai Minister was involved in a fracas over a parked car with one of the more irascible French delegates which would – if Stephen had not intervened – have resulted in another display of Thai-style boxing, and the General unexpectedly had to go to Cheing Mei, a town in the north of the country, which meant telescoping their final afternoon session with him into a couple of hours in the morning.

By late afternoon Julia felt as if all her nerves had been exposed to a dentist's drill, and with relief she returned home to pack the few things she would need for her week's stay in London. If it were not for Nick's packages she could have managed with a week-end holdall. She stared in exasperation at the grinning Buddhas and long-stemmed pipes waiting to fit between her slippers and dressing-gown. Woe betide her if she was to break any of his gifts in transit.

Hospitable as ever, Mrs. Rogers had decided to give Stephen a farewell dinner, but had diplomatically not invited Kim, feeling this would be an ordeal with which Julia could no longer cope. Yet oddly enough Julia had felt apathetic about seeing him; she seemed to be living in limbo, all her emotions suspended so that the person moving and talking and saying the right thing at the right time was only the shadow of herself.

Yet even the shadow was capable of feeling pain at the sight of May-lin standing close to Stephen and smiling at him with eyes that remembered too much.

Dinner was an ordeal to be endured and she picked at her food, murmuring – as she met Mrs. Rogers's worried eyes – that she had a headache. It gave her an excuse to go to bed early, for making small talk was totally beyond her ability to-night. The thought of the long flight ahead with Stephen loomed as a further ordeal to be endured, and she was determined to sit as far away from him as possible. With the other delegates returning on the same plane it should be possible to avoid him completely.

In London and Brussels they would be thrown together more closely than ever, and she prayed for the strength not to give herself away. How could she love a man who didn't know she existed except as a capable work-horse? And equally important, how could she love a man who had not come to terms with himself? Whose very faults she abhorred? Yet those faults made him the person he was; gave him the idiosyncrasies and foibles she found so touching. But she must not think of him. She must put him out of her mind. Quickening her pace as though she could run away from her thoughts, she sped down the corridor.

A plump man stepped back in time to prevent colliding with her, and with a gasp she stopped and apologised. It was Sako, the Thai valet whom the British Embassy had assigned to look after Stephen. His usually impassive countenance was marked by a frown which lightened as he unloaded his problem on to her. Mr. Brandon had succumbed to the many beautiful things one could buy in Thailand and had bought so many gifts that packing them had been a nightmare.

"I have managed to get them all in except one," he concluded, "and that is too big to fit in anywhere."

"Make it into a separate parcel."

"Mr. Brandon does not like to carry parcels."

"I'm sure he'll make an exception this time," Julia said, considering the matter a storm in a tea-cup.

But Sako refused to be pacified, and moving to one side, motioned Julia to see the cause of the trouble for herself.

Surveying the square, gold-wrapped package on the bed, she appreciated the valet's difficulty. It was certainly too festive-looking for Stephen to carry himself, since to the photographers who would undoubtedly be awaiting for him at London Airport, it would look as if he had returned with a Christmas present!

She lifted the package and shook it gingerly. "If there are several small objects in here you might be able to fit them in."

"You mean undo it?" Sako looked dubious. "It might be a special present for someone. It was on the bed among the other gifts when I came in to pack."

"Then you'd better wait and ask Mr. Brandon what to do."

Anxious to leave, she moved to the door, but Sako appeared so crestfallen that she decided to take matters into her own hands. Returning to the bed, she tore off the gold paper, to disclose a thick, beautifully carved picture frame holding the smiling face of the General. The words, "In grateful appreciation for so much help," were penned at the bottom.

"Well, you certainly can't divide that!" she said humorously, and looked at the bulging case on the floor. "I'd better put it in *my* bag. I've plenty of room."

In the morning there was the usual rush of departure. The airport was bursting with people, but the magic of diplomatic passports and the presence of the British Vice-Consul whisked them through the formalities, though it could not prevent their luggage being examined in the Customs Hall.

Stephen appeared regardless of the unusually detailed examination his cases received, though from the strained expression on the Vice-Consul's face Julia knew a letter of protest would that afternoon be winging its way from one Embassy to another.

"I've already told you I've nothing to declare," Stephen said haughtily, when a pile of pure silk shirts were roughly undone.

"Forgive me, sir. It is only a formality."

The sibilant voice was accompanied by a nervous smile as the man stepped aside to let another one take his place. Taller than his companion, the gold on his lapels indicated his superior position, which he now exercised by going through Stephen's cases again.

"*What* are you looking for?" the Vice-Consul demanded. "Mr. Brandon has a plane to catch. Surely it isn't necessary to examine luggage so carefully on the way *out* of your country?"

"Regrettably it is. Your students have made it so."

"What have our students got to do with Mr. Brandon?"

A shrug lifted the official's shoulders, then, as though coming to a decision, he re-opened Julia's case and began to go through every item again. Each one of Nick's articles was taken out of its paper and examined; irritating to watch, it became embarrassing when a chiffon nightdress was held up to the light.

"Perhaps he's looking for code writing on the bodice!" Stephen whispered, his good humour returning.

The official lifted a pink linen jacket and underneath, wrapped in tissue paper, lay the elaborate picture frame and the smiling portrait of the General. Reverently the man picked it up. He was obviously an admirer of the General and impressed by what he believed to be a show of the General's affection towards this lovely English girl.

As Stephen saw the photograph one of his eyebrows raised, and Julia knew that Sako had not told him he had given it to her to carry. She moved over to explain, but a muttered oath made her stop. Turning, she saw blunt fingers tapping the thick, carved edge of the frame.

"It's a perfectly ordinary picture frame," she said loudly. "There's no need to open it."

"Forgive me," the man said, but went on examining it.

As though her anger was contagious Stephen left the Vice-Consul's side and stepped over to the counter again. As he did so the edge of the picture frame fell away.

"Now you've broken it!" Julia exclaimed. "Can't you – "

The words died in her throat as the man set one half of the frame on the counter and from the other half removed an oilskin package some eight inches square and an inch thick. Carefully he unwound the oilskin and sniffed the white powder it had been covering.

"What on earth is that?" she gasped.

The man looked at her; a cold, hard look that she found unexpectedly terrifying.

"Please follow me."

"Why? I haven't done anything wrong. I don't know what that stuff is."

She flung a beseeching look at Stephen and the horror on his face made her own fear intensify. Why was he staring at her like that?

"What is it?" she cried again. "What's that powder?"

"Marijuana," Stephen said harshly. "You'd better go with the officer. I'll follow in a moment."

Unable to believe this was happening to her, she followed the man into a small room with a barred window. Marijuana in the picture frame! It was unbelievable. One read about such a thing in a book or a newspaper, but it was not something that happened to a person one knew. 'But it's happening to *me*!' she thought wildly. 'To me!'

What subtlety of mind Stephen had shown to hide the drug behind the General's photograph! And a signed picture too, which made it seem as if the frame itself was part of the gift.

But why had he done such a crazy thing? It was certainly not because he needed the money. Yet what other reason did he have?

Devilment? Excitement?

With a clarity engendered by stark fear she remembered something he had said one night at a dinner party – the night of Nick's arrival in Bangkok.

"There's nothing more exciting than pitting your wits against authority," he had asserted. "Once you have all the money you need, the only thing you're scared of losing is your reputation."

So many brave words, she had thought at the time, but now they returned to haunt her. He had probably been planning this very escapade when he had been talking that night.

Psychologically impelled to prove himself all the time, he could only find peace of mind by putting his courage to the test. And each test had to be more dangerous; the line between failure and success becoming so fine that it would eventually topple him over into disaster.

As it had done today. Except that the disaster was hers, for she had been carrying the picture frame!

Anger flooded through her as she realised the outcome of his crazy behaviour. To court danger for yourself was one thing, but when your failure could destroy the Trade Talks, then you were committing an act of folly almost amounting to treason!

Yet that was what he had done. And by failing in his mad scheme, he had given the General's enemies all the ammunition they needed.

Everyone knew Stephen and General Banton were friends, and smuggling drugs in a picture frame given to him by the General might very well implicate the man himself. In a country like this, where rumour could be blown up into scandal, and scandal could bring down a government, such an allegation could well lead to the General's downfall.

The door opened and Stephen came in accompanied by two officers.

"What's happening?" Julia asked, surprised to find that her voice came out as a whisper.

"They're detaining you." He came closer. "What in the name of heaven did *you* have to take it for?"

"I didn't know what was in it. If I had, I'd have destroyed it! I didn't know," she repeated.

"You'll have a job proving it."

"*You* know the truth. You've got to get me out."

"I'll do my best," he said, "but it will take time and a lot of influence. Don't you realise what this means? It could ruin everything we've worked for! You're my secretary – part of the delegation . . . and then putting a signed photo of the General in the frame as well. . . . A thing like that could crucify him!"

Julia stared at Stephen, unable to believe her ears. Surely he wasn't going to let *her* carry the guilt for what he had done?

"I know exactly what it can do to the General," she cried, "but you can't let *me* take the blame! If I hadn't – "

"Julia!" Stephen gripped her shoulders so tightly that she was silenced. Still holding her, he looked up at the lamp dangling from the ceiling. "It's bugged," he said into her ear. "Be careful what you say."

Be careful not to implicate *him*, she thought bitterly, and wrenched herself free. "You're the one who should be careful!" she flared.

"I'm trying to be. It isn't my own reputation I'm thinking of, it's the success of everything we've been working for this last month. I'll pull every string I can to get you out of this, but it may take time. I'll talk to the General. He'll want to help you – for my sake if not for yours – but he'll have to go slowly."

"Will you tell him the truth?"

"There's no point. It won't make any difference to his trying to help. He'll do that anyway."

"So you'll let him think *I'm* guilty?"

"Will that worry you so long as you're free? Surely that's the most important thing?"

"I care about my reputation."

"You care about somebody else's reputation even more," he said softly, "otherwise you'd have said the frame wasn't yours when they opened it."

"You know very well why I kept quiet."

Lines etched themselves either side of his mouth, giving him an unfamiliar, brooding look. "Yes," he replied. "I do."

Behind him the two officers moved restlessly, and he went to the door. "Try not to worry." He hesitated and one hand, half raised to her, became a clenched fist. "What a fool you are!" he said. "If only you hadn't taken it."

The door closed behind him and in the small cubicle of a room Julia felt more alone than at any time in her life.

CHAPTER ELEVEN

"GONE? I don't believe it. Stephen wouldn't go and leave me!"

"He had no choice," said the Vice-Consul. "He had to make his report to the Prime Minister and then go to Brussels. Everything was arranged. But he should be back within ten days."

Ten more days of prison. Julia stared at the wooden table in front of her. She had been brought to this stiflingly hot waiting-room by a prison guard who had told her she had a visitor and, expecting Stephen, had been dismayed to find Mr. Fitzharding. Her first thought – that Stephen was too busy trying to get her release to come and see her – had been destroyed when she had learned he had left the country. And without even coming to say good-bye or sending her a note.

"What's going to happen to me?" she whispered. "I'm not guilty, Mr. Fitzharding. I didn't put that marijuana in the frame. The frame doesn't even – "

"I *know*." The Vice-Consul interrupted with such vehemence that she looked at him in surprise and saw that, like Stephen had done in the room at the airport a few days ago, he was staring at the lamp above their heads.

"Do they listen to *everything* we say?" she mouthed.

The grey head nodded and she fell silent. Had Stephen confessed to the Vice-Consul that the frame was his? Only this would explain Mr. Fitzharding's fear that she might say too much, for he too was concerned with the success of the trade talks and would rather have *her* name ruined than Stephen's. After all, what did the reputation of an English secretary matter compared with the commerce and industry that would result from Stephen's negotiations?

"They imprison people for smuggling," she said huskily. "That's why they've brought me here."

"We are doing our best to obtain your release, but these things take time. Mr. Brandon was unable to see the General before he left, but he spoke to him on the telephone."

"That was good of him," she said dryly, and saw Mr. Fitzharding look at her with such surprise that she wondered if Stephen had told him the truth after all. Perhaps the man really did think she had put the drugs into the frame?

"What happens if you can't get my release?" she asked. "The Thais are hard on drug smugglers, aren't they?"

"More against 'hard drugs' than 'soft ones'."

"But I could still go to prison?"

"I am sure we can avoid that eventually. We think it will be a question of a heavy fine, but Mr. Brandon has already told me he will pay whatever is necessary."

"How generous of him!"

This time Julia's sarcasm was too heavy for the Vice-Consul to ignore. "It is very generous indeed. Your behaviour could have wrecked – " he glanced above his head and stopped abruptly. "If there's anything you would like, please get in touch with me."

"If they're going to fine me," she said quickly, "why can't they get it over with?"

"In the normal course of events you would have to stand trial, but Mr. Brandon is hoping the General will prevent this. It's all most unfortunate."

"It would have been even more unfortunate if Mr. Brandon – " Julia also remembered to stop in time. "But you'd better ask *him* to explain – if he will!"

Hurriedly pushing back his chair, the Vice-Consul bade her a hasty goodbye and left.

The prison to which Julia had been taken was newly built, though the air-conditioning had a tendency to go off unexpectedly. She had a tiny room to herself – unlike the other women who were packed three and four to a cell – and wondered if her seclusion was due to Stephen's influence or because she was a foreigner.

A few of the guards spoke a smattering of English, but their sing-song tone, so much a part of the Thai language itself, made it difficult for her to understand them. Their attitude was friendly though wary, and she felt they knew that everything they said was being monitored. It was unnerving to accept that every word spoken was being inexorably recorded on a magnetic band. Was there a room somewhere in this building where men sat day and night listening to every sound the prisoners made? The tears, the laughter, the reiteration of innocence or the defiant assertion of guilt?

A few more months in this atmosphere and it would be easy for her to believe she too was guilty, Julia mused one night as she lay on her hard bunk. She forced herself to re-live that last evening at home when, in an effort to help the valet she had unwrapped the gold package and put the frame in her own case. What would she have done had she discovered its hidden contents? Would she have taken it to Stephen and accused him of criminal stupidity, or would she have flushed the powder down the sink and taken the empty frame through the Customs, giving it triumphantly to him on her return to London?

For the hundredth time she wondered how he had felt when his suitcases had been so thoroughly searched without the picture frame being found. And what had he thought when he had seen it in her own case? His subsequent behaviour had given her no clue. All she knew was that he had not told anyone that the frame was his, that he was going to let her take the blame.

This belief was confirmed when Mrs. Rogers called to see her at the end of the week. Like a breath of sanity the woman breezed into the visitors' room, enveloping Julia in a warm embrace. She had obviously been warned to be careful what she said, for though she chattered volubly, it was all idle gossip.

Only as she was leaving did Julia herself bring some reality into the conversation. Clutching at Mrs. Rogers's arm, she leaned close to her.

"I'm innocent," she whispered. "The frame wasn't mine."

"I know."

Julia's heart beat faster. "Did Stephen tell you?"

"Yes. He said you were protecting someone."

"Didn't he tell you *who*?"

Mrs. Rogers nodded and Julia gave a sigh of relief, her disillusionment dissolving like mist in sunshine.

"He was furious with you, of course," the woman went on. "I never realised he could get so angry with anyone."

"He should be more angry with himself."

"I don't see why. He wasn't to blame."

The guard looked meaningly at his watch, and taking the hint before it could be verbalised, Mrs. Rogers hugged Julia and left.

Alone again, Julia pondered over Mrs. Rogers's last words. Why should Stephen be so angry with her when her actions had safeguarded him? Or did he still believe that if the frame had been found in his own case the Customs official would not have examined it so closely?

No matter how long she considered these questions she could not find an answer, and her desire to be free grew stronger. Her hope of being released by the end of the week came to nothing, and though she pestered the guards to know what was happening, they merely smiled and shook their heads.

The week-end seemed never-ending. No visitors were allowed and the prison was as silent as a graveyard. Late on Sunday evening when Julia was sunk into the depths of despair, a guard once more came to escort her to the waiting room, and entering it, her listlessness vanished as she saw Kim.

"I had to see you, Julia. I could not keep away any longer."

Uncertain how to reply, for he did not come forward to greet her, she too kept her distance and waited for him to continue.

"Why did you do it?" he burst out. "You're not a drug

smuggler. I don't believe it! You're protecting someone, aren't you?"

His belief in her innocence warmed her, but though she longed to tell him the truth she could not do so. They had different loyalties and – even more important – he was one of General Banton's aides. To tell him she was protecting Stephen could destroy everything that the Delegation had worked to achieve.

"Tell me whom you're protecting," Kim reiterated.

"No one."

"I don't believe you. You're innocent, Julia. You can't fool *me*!"

Still forcing herself to hide her joy at his faith in her, she kept her voice calm as she told him firmly that the frame *was* hers.

"But I didn't put the marijuana in it," she said, determined to get this point across to the police who were no doubt monitoring the conversation. "Someone else did *that*."

"The picture frame *wasn't* yours," Kim insisted.

"It was! The General gave me his picture and I – and I bought a frame for it."

"Where did you buy it?"

"I don't remember. I went to a lot of shops before I found what I wanted."

"You are foolish crazy to go on lying," Kim said. "You could go to prison for seven years. Our laws are harsh, Julia, for heaven's sake be realistic."

"I'm telling you the truth. The frame was mine, but I never put anything inside it. Never!"

"You are protecting someone else," Kim said once again, and walked heavily to the door.

On the threshold he looked back at her, opened his mouth as though to say something more, and then went out.

Julia bit back a sigh. If only she could have told Kim the truth; loving her and believing in her innocence, the way he did, it seemed wrong not to do so. Yet to admit Stephen's guilt would be disclosing an aspect of his character that made her ashamed for him. What a pity he did not appear to have the same shame for himself! Was the strong love-hate relationship he felt for his mother – and for which he was still so desperately guilty – impelling him to destroy himself? Like all the questions that had been plaguing her, this too could not be answered, though it did not stop her from returning to it during the next few days.

Despite the extra food sent to her by the Vice-Consul, lack of exercise made it difficult for her to eat even the normal ration of rice, and she gazed longingly at the bright sunshine through the narrow window of her cell. Exercise was kept to a minimum, as was conversation, and one boring day melted into another. Her only consolation – that Nick knew nothing of what had happened – received a rude jolt when one of the guards handed her a telegram from him.

"Just seen report your arrest. Stop. Willing return unless can help in England. Stop. Cable American Express Hamburg. Stop. Know you're innocent. Love Nick."

Brief though the message was it cheered her enormously, and afraid that at this very moment he might be preparing to return to Thailand, she wrote out a reply and handed it to the guard.

"The British Consul will pay," she explained. "I have no money."

The man looked at the sheet of paper doubtfully. "You not wish husband come here?"

"It isn't my husband, it's my brother."

"I give message to Inspector. He must read first."

"Send it as quickly as you can," she pleaded, giving him her most brilliant smile. "It's very urgent."

Within an hour the guard returned to tell her the telegram had been despatched, and though unsure if this was true, she pretended to believe him. For all their charm and easy manner the Thais were proud and quick-tempered, and to doubt their word could lead to an eruption of awesome violence. It might have been better if she had tried to call Mrs. Rogers and ask *her* to send Nick the telegram. But it was too late to do anything about it now, and she read and re-read her brother's message, hoping he would receive her reply and continue on his way to England.

Several more days dragged by. The bloom left Julia's cheeks though her hair glowed vibrant as ever, almost as if all her spirit were contained in it.

The guards were intrigued by her appearance, and one of them in particular made no secret of his admiration. Whenever he came on duty he bought her a small gift: a slice of pineapple wrapped in a plastic bag – always available on the streets of Bangkok; a packet of sugary sweets or a sticky dessert of glutinous rice wrapped in a banana leaf. This latter gift required great effort for her to eat, but unwilling to offend him, she would pretend to enjoy it, sucking her fingers and smiling at him as she did so; an act which always made him grin widely.

At the end of the second week the Vice-Consul called to see her again.

"No more news, I fear," he said. "General Banton is still in Cheing Mei, and nothing can be done until he returns to Bangkok. Our main effort is to make sure you aren't brought to trial before then."

"Is that likely?"

"No, no," he said, too quickly for her comfort. "Once the General is in Bangkok I'm sure he will obtain your release."

"And then what happens to me?" she interrupted.

"You will be sent to England."

Only then did Julia realise how, in protecting Stephen, she had ruined her own future. Gone was any hope of returning here to work with Mrs. Rogers. And what chance did she have of getting a decent position at home? People would be wary of employing someone who had been convicted of drug smuggling. Even the very words filled her with revulsion.

What would Stephen have done with the drug once he had

got it safely through the Customs? Probably dumped it some-where in the sea, she thought, or taken it to the drug squad at Scotland Yard and told them how easy it was to get it out of one country and into another!

"Don't look so despondent, my dear," Mr. Fitzharding said, reminding her that he was still with her.

She gave him an absentminded smile and was glad when, having delivered himself of a further peroration, he departed. Returning to her cell, she decided she felt better when she had no visitors at all, for being able to talk to someone in her own language only increased her loneliness when they had gone.

Depression was still with her when, an hour later, she was again led back to the visitors' room. Who was it this time, she asked herself despondently, Mrs. Rogers or Kim? Not Kim, she prayed. She could not face more of his persistent question-ing.

Entering the room, she stopped abruptly, her heart pounding at sight of the tall thin figure standing by the window.

Stephen! He had come back to her again.

He swung round to look at her, and as his face came into focus – the dark eyes glittering, the brows almost touching in a frown of anger – she drew back.

"Stephen! When did you . . . Mr. Fitzharding never said a word!"

"He didn't know. I flew in an hour ago and came here straight from the airport." His words held the same fury as his ex-pression, his drawl replaced by a sharp urgency she had never heard before.

"I saw Nick," he went on harshly. "He got your telegram and came to see me the minute he arrived in England. He wanted to know what had happened."

"Did you tell him the truth?"

"The truth!" he burst out. "That's what *I've* come here to find. I wasn't due back till next week, but after seeing Nick I flew out at once." Her perplexity showed in her face and he took

146

an angry step towards her. "For heaven's sake, Julia, what game are you playing?"

Unable to understand what he was talking about, she played for time, careful to remember that their conversation was being overheard.

"I've already told you why I'm doing it."

"It doesn't make sense." Stephen kept his voice as low as possible. "You didn't know about the marijuana in the frame, did you?"

Julia glanced round her, fearful lest a television eye had been planted in the room apart from a microphone. Then without speaking, she shook her head.

"Then where did you get the frame?" he asked. "You've got to tell me."

His question was so incredible that she wondered if she was living in a nightmare. Or was he trying to tell her he was willing to take the blame? And what would happen to the trade negotiations if he did?

For the first time she wondered if the talks had foundered; this could be the only logical explanation.

Testing her theory, she said: "Did you go to Brussels?"

"Of course." He seemed surprised by her question. "That's one of the reasons I had to fly home."

"Is everything all right?"

"Naturally. There are still several points to be settled, but they shouldn't be insuperable."

"Then you mustn't let anything prevent the agreement being ratified," she said firmly.

"Do you think you need bother telling me that?" he asked irritably.

"It looks as if I must. The treaty is as important now as it was a couple of weeks ago. What happens to me doesn't matter. Mr. Fitzharding said you'd pay any fine necessary. He was sure your friendship with the General would help you to get my release."

"Is that all you care about?" he asked. "Aren't you upset at being branded a smuggler?"

She avoided his glance; so his conscience was troubling him after all! He obviously wanted to be sure she would forgive him for letting her shoulder the guilt that was rightfully his. More than anything else he had done, this sign of his weakness filled her with bitterness; poor Stephen. He had to be approved of no matter how badly he had behaved.

"My good name isn't as important as yours," she murmured.

"What's that got to do with it?"

"Everything!" She shouted the word, giving him the answer she knew he had been wanting to hear since he had come into the room. "I'm sticking to my story, Stephen," she repeated, "so go away and leave me alone."

Her anger seemed to absorb his, for the fury left his face, leaving it pale and haggard. "It's love, I suppose," he said softly.

She nodded. Pride was no longer important; it had been destroyed by her solitary weeks in prison. "Yes," she whispered, "it's love."

"Are you quite sure you won't have any regrets?"

"Positive."

He sighed. "It can never mean marriage. You do understand that? In the eyes of the world you'll be guilty, and that will rule out marriage completely."

"I never expected marriage."

"Then you're an even bigger fool than I took you for!" Angrily he strode to the door. "I brought you some books," he went on in a tight voice, and walked out before she could reply.

His steps receded into the distance, and the silence that followed seeped away her reserve like so much sand in the tide. After a few moments she went to the door and knocked on it to attract the attention of a guard. But no one came to collect her, and remembering that the guards often had a habit of disappearing on mysterious errands of their own, she returned to the chair and sat down.

The parcel Stephen had brought her lay on the table and numbly she opened it, looking without emotion at the books inside. They were all non-fiction and light reading, as though deliberately chosen to stop her from thinking. If only it were as easy as that!

She shook her head. Stephen did not want her to think. If she did, she would only despise him. Anger welled up in her. How dared he come here and put on such an act? Even though she guessed he had done it to hoodwink the authorities she still hated him for being cold-blooded enough to do so. Remembering what he had said she marvelled that she had been able to control her temper. Though he could not have admitted his guilt, nor even hinted at an apology while there was the slightest risk of his being overheard, there had been no need for him to taunt her because she loved him.

Bitterness seeped through her again, and angrily she flung the parcel of books to the floor. She wanted nothing from Stephen; neither his pity, his understanding or his help. Indeed she would rather remain in prison for ever than have him buy her freedom! Once more she went over and banged on the door. But there was still no response and she paced the room.

Through the narrow window the last rays of the setting sun sent a ribbon of gold across the concrete floor. It picked out the scuff marks on the legs of the wooden table and the dents in the side of the chair, as if someone had flung it down with the same anger that she had flung down the books. She bent to retrieve them and, doing so, noticed the glint of the gold paper in which they had been wrapped.

Inexplicably she was reminded of the golden roof of the temple she had so blithely photographed several weeks ago. How carefree she had been then – unaware of the ordeal that lay ahead of her. She even remembered the last time she had used her camera: the night of General Banton's party at the Siam Intercontinental Hotel, when she had been walking in the grounds and had nearly found herself face to face with May-lin.

Idly Julia smoothed the paper and re-wrapped it round the books. May-lin had been holding a gold package identical to this one, she recollected, as large and square as the picture frame.

The picture frame . . . .

A wild and fanciful thought came into her mind, so fanciful that she dismissed it at once. It was crazy to think such a thing. Yet crazy or not, the idea grew so strong and insistent she decided not to fight it any more, but to concentrate on it, knowing she must either find a way of giving it credence or be able to dismiss it for ever.

But the more she thought of it the more it refused to be dismissed, and questions she had never considered before began to demand answers. Who had given May-lin that large gold package, and what if it *had* held the picture frame? Could May-lin have then given it to Stephen? And if so surely she had known it had a secret compartment. Yet this meant she had known about Stephen's planned escapade.

Julia frowned. Stephen would never have confided in anyone. The very premise on which he courted danger would have prevented him asking anyone for help: the danger had to be entirely his. Therefore May-lin could not have been involved. Yet the parcel she had held had looked identical to the one Julia had found on Stephen's bed. Not that this was significant in a country where gold wrapping was as common as brown paper was in England!

Even as she thought this, another more subtle one came to mind. Suppose May-lin was involved and Stephen wasn't?

Once again Julia frowned. Was her jealousy of May-lin making her find the girl guilty, or was her reasoning – which had led her to this point – based on sound, logical fact?

Fact, Julia decided firmly, not jealousy. The fact of a gold-wrapped package identical in shape and size to the picture frame. It might all be the long arm of coincidence, but it was pointing to a question that had to be answered.

Could Stephen be innocent?

It was the first time Julia had considered this possibility, and she explored it tentatively. If Stephen had wanted to hide marijuana in a picture frame he would not have asked May-lin to get him one. That was something she had already decided. Therefore she must look at events from another angle: from May-lin's point of view.

What if the girl had given Stephen the frame as a present and someone *else* had hidden the drug inside it? If it were discovered – and the scrutiny his luggage had received at the Customs indicated that someone had warned them in the hope that this would be so – then it showed a deliberate plot to smear his name. The reason required no great deduction: destroy his image and the trade talks would be destroyed too.

Until this moment Julia had believed Stephen to be guilty and, believing it, everything had made sense. Yet if she took the opposite view things *still* made sense. More so, in fact, for many of the inexplicable things he had said to her this afternoon became understandable: his fury at the way she had answered his questions; his admission that he had returned here immediately after speaking to Nick – as though Nick had given him fresh impetus to talk to her. But what could Nick have told him?

Carefully she went over everything Stephen had said, then forced herself to think back to their conversation before he had left Thailand. Memory returned with difficulty, but she was able to recall enough to convince her she was approaching a solution.

Stephen had accused her of protecting someone. And if he himself was innocent, then he could only have been referring to Nick. Certainly he would never think she would want to protect May-lin!

Excitement sent Julia pacing the floor. Stephen had been in the hall when Nick had dumped some packages in her arms and asked her to take them back to England for him. What was more obvious than for Stephen to assume one of those packages to have been the picture frame? And when he had seen it in her case he had immediately associated it with Nick – the word student so often being synonymous with drugs.

Believing she was protecting her brother, Stephen had returned to England, and not until he had seen Nick himself and learned that he was innocent, had he wondered who else she could be protecting.

What a fool she had been not to realise all this when he had so angrily asked her that very question. It had not only been his way of telling her he knew Nick was blameless, but also of trying to find out *who* had given her the frame in the first place! His fury at her refusal to tell him – which had made no sense at all at the time – now showed one thing very clearly: his own unawareness that she had been protecting him!

This brought her face to face with the only possible solution: someone had planted the frame on Stephen. And suspicion pointed to May-lin.

But why would May-lin want to destroy Stephen's reputation? The difficulty of answering the question seemed likely to be as arduous as the reasoning which had brought her to this point, and she forced herself to remain calm. Only by doing so would she find the answer.

CHAPTER TWELVE

FOR what seemed an interminable length of time Julia tried to make sense out of a situation that seemed senseless. Had May-lin wanted to destroy Stephen's reputation because he had not asked her to marry him? Yet he had said she was leaving Thailand, and Julia had assumed this to mean she was going to live in England. If this were true, the whole edifice on which she had built Stephen's innocence collapsed, leaving her back where she had started.

But she wouldn't let herself go back to that premise. Stephen was innocent. She must go on believing that. Someone wanted to make him look guilty, and she was convinced it was May-lin.

Yet if there was no personal reason – and Stephen's attentions towards the girl ruled this out – then her motivation could only be political.

But how could such an exquisite creature, whose family tree had been sheltered from the winds of deprivation for centuries, be a Communist? The idea was ludicrous, yet. . . .

Yet Communism was an ideology that appealed to all ranks and all levels; and if it had attracted May-lin, it would provide the reason for her actions. And how clever those actions had been!

She had been a guest in Mrs. Rogers' house the night before Stephen had left Bangkok, so it would have been easy for her to put the package in his bedroom. She had even had the foresight to wonder what would happen if he saw it before his valet had packed it, and had cleverly put a photograph of the General in the frame, knowing Stephen would immediately assume it to be an unexpected gift from his friend.

The feverish excitement which had buoyed Julia up suddenly subsided. Her reasoning was sound, but how on earth could she prove it?

Unexpectedly she remembered Stephen's cruel jibe that the man she was protecting would never marry her now that she had ruined her reputation. At the time she had seen the remark as a warning from Stephen not to expect gratitude for saving his reputation. But if he was innocent then this remark made no sense unless. . . .

With a cry of triumph she jumped to her feet. Though she still lacked proof of May-lin's guilt, she could at least work out why Stephen thought she herself had willingly gone to prison! After talking to Nick and realising she was not protecting her brother, he had automatically thought she was protecting the only other man she might care for: Kim.

Julia's breath – coming as fast as her thoughts – was equally uncontrollable. If Stephen believed this, then every single thing he had said made sense.

Again her thoughts returned to May-lin. There must be some way of proving the girl had had the package. Carefully she cast her mind back to the night of the General's party when she had seen May-lin – half hidden by shrubbery – take a gold-wrapped parcel from a man in the same instant that she herself had taken a photograph of the hotel. Julia frowned. Could she have photographed May-lin too? Would the package have been visible through the eye of the lens? She must have thought so at the time because she remembered being irritated at having to take a second photograph.

And both of them were still unexposed in her camera.

"I've got to develop that roll of film," Julia thought. Only when she saw what was on it would she be able to decide her next move. But first she must get the camera from Mrs. Rogers' house. Not anticipating she would want it during her week in London she had luckily left it behind on the fateful day of her departure.

Running to the door, she pounded on it, keeping up the noise until eventually slow steps marked the approach of a guard. A key turned in the lock and facing her was a morose-looking man she had not seen before.

Assuming she wished to return to her cell, he gestured her to move, but she remained where she was and mimed that she wanted to make a telephone call. Shaking his head, he caught her arm and pushed her along the corridor.

"I want to speak to Mr. Brandon," she protested.

A spate of Thai was her only answer, and knowing that if she stepped inside her cell she would be lost, she obstinately remained on the threshold.

"I *must* speak to Mr. Brandon! It's very important."

Her reiteration had the opposite effect from what she had hoped, for with an exclamation the guard began to push her into the cell.

"Then let me talk to Major Chan," she cried, bracing her feet against the floor. "He works with General Banton."

The guard's expression changed from anger to dubiousness and she pressed home her advantage. "I want to talk to Major Chan. Major Kim Chan!"

Muttering angrily, the man closed the door on her and immediately she started to pound on it. Never had she felt so helpless and angry. It was a frightening combination of emotions – the one adding to the other until all reason vanished and she was caught in a spiral of terror that seemed never-ending. Only the sight of her hands, raw and red from beating against the woodwork, brought her back to sanity, and she sank on to the bed and forced herself to think calmly.

She would not be left here alone indefinitely. Sooner or later she would be allowed a visitor and . . . her breath caught on a sob. She couldn't sit here and wait. She had to get that camera. It was her only hope.

The sound of the door opening brought her to her feet, and only as the light came on did she realise that darkness had fallen. A slim figure came toward her, and unused to the brightness she blinked her eyes, relief flooding through her as she saw who it was.

"Kim!" she cried. "Thank goodness you've come. I wanted to call Stephen, but they wouldn't let me."

Kim caught her shoulders in a reassuring grip. "What is it, Julia?"

"I know who planted the marijuana in the frame!"

"Who planted it?" Startled, Kim's hands dropped to his sides.

"Yes. You said you believed I was innocent and now I can prove it. I know who put the frame in Stephen's room."

"So it *was* Stephen!" Kim said loudly. "You were smuggling it out of the country for *him?*"

"Of course not," she said, irritated by his obtuseness. "I found it in his room, but it wasn't *his.* He didn't know anything about it. It had been put there to implicate him!"

"Why would anyone want to do that?"

"To discredit him and ruin the trade talks. You know what a scandal it would have caused if he'd been caught smuggling drugs."

"But how did *you* get the frame?"

"By accident. I was going to bed when Sako – Stephen's valet – saw me. He said he didn't have room to pack one last parcel and he didn't like asking Stephen to carry it. I offered to put it in my case instead. Stephen never even saw it."

"How can you be sure? If anyone planted it in his room they were taking an awful chance. Say he'd gone upstairs before the valet had finished packing? He wouldn't just have ignored it – unless he was in the habit of getting gold-wrapped gifts!"

"That's where the whole thing's so clever," Julia said, ignoring the sarcasm. "Using the General's picture made it foolproof. Don't you see that? If Stephen *had* found the frame, once he saw the General's photo he'd have assumed it had come from *him.*"

"As a present, you mean?" Kim said dubiously. "Even so. . . ."

"I'm *right!*" she burst out. "It was sheer accident that I bumped into Sako and took the frame from him. If I hadn't,

Stephen would have been carrying it instead of me."

Kim's eyes were shadowed as though with pain. "So all this time you've been protecting him?"

"Yes." She hurried over the word. "But now I can tell the truth. The frame doesn't belong to either of us."

"You might find that hard to prove," Kim said gravely. "All you've done so far is to show how despicably Brandon's behaved in letting you take the blame for him."

"But he doesn't know!" she cried. "He never *saw* the frame till the Customs man took it out of my case. That's what I'm trying to tell you. It was planted on him by May-lin!"

"May-lin!" Kim looked utterly astounded. "You can't be serious?"

"I'm not in the mood for joking," Julia said bitterly. "May-lin planted the frame in Stephen's room the night before we were due to leave Bangkok. She had dinner at the house and plenty of opportunity to go upstairs without being seen."

"But it doesn't make sense. I'd always assumed she and Stephen were — " Kim sought and found the right euphemism, "were very good friends. Why would she *do* it?"

"Because she's a Communist."

Kim burst out laughing. "You can't expect me to believe *that*! Her family is one of the most respected in Thailand."

"I don't care if it's the most respected in the world!" Julia said tersely. "She's a Communist."

"Never!"

"She planted that picture frame," Julia reiterated. "I saw her get it."

Again she had the satisfaction of seeing Kim look astounded. "You *saw* May-lin get it! When was this?"

"The night of General Banton's party. It was in the grounds of the hotel. I'd gone out to take some pictures and saw May-lin talking to a man."

"A man!" There was no doubting Kim's interest now. His whole face was alive with it, his body trembling as eagerly as hers. "Did you see who it was?"

Julia shook her head. "They were hidden by shrubs. But May-lin moved and I saw the man give her a package – the picture frame."

Kim's narrow shoulders lifted, the gesture showing – far more than words – that his excitement had ebbed. "It won't work, Julia. It was a good try, but you'd never convince anyone on such flimsy evidence. What if someone *did* give her a parcel? It could have been anything!"

"It was identical to the parcel on the bed."

"It would be your word against hers."

"Not just my word," Julia said quietly. "I've got evidence. A picture in my camera."

Kim's breath hissed through his teeth like a jet of gas, and triumphantly she nodded. "It's true! I was taking some shots that night – I told you – and I didn't realise I'd photographed May-lin until it was too late. She took the package just as I clicked the shutter. It's come out on the film."

"In the dark?" Kim said incredulously. "For heaven's sake don't pin your hopes on *that*!"

"It wasn't complete darkness," Julia said with far more conviction than she felt. "The moon came out just as I took the shot."

"Even so . . . ." he frowned. "Say you *did* get May-lin and the package, you'll never prove it was wrapped in gold paper."

"I *can*. Develop the film and you'll see for yourself. You've got to help me, Kim. It's my only chance of proving Stephen and I are innocent."

Kim came and stood close to her, their eyes level. "I hate to see you build your hopes on such flimsy . . . ." he sighed. "Where is your camera?"

"In my bedroom in Mrs. Rogers' house. If you telephone Stephen I'm sure he'd – "

"I'd rather do it myself," Kim interrupted decisively. "I have a meeting with the General in half an hour's time, but I'll go the moment it's over."

The relief that something was going to be done at last was so overwhelming that for a moment Julia was speechless. Recognising her emotion, Kim put his hand on hers, his face concerned.

"Please, my dear, don't be so certain."

"I *am* certain." Refusing to consider doubt, she swung to assertion. "I don't know if the house is open. I think Mrs. Rogers has gone to Pattaya for a few days.

"She has a night-watchman. It shouldn't be difficult to get in."

"Can't you go now?"

"And keep the General waiting? He'd have my head off!" Kim smiled. "I'll go the moment I'm free. Don't worry, my dear."

He hesitated, looked as if he were going to kiss her, and then changed his mind and squeezed her hand again before going to the door and rapping on it to signify he wished to leave.

Alone again, Julia's excitement gradually faded, leaving her with a feeling of emptiness. Anticipation, with nothing to feed on except itself, could not be sustained for long and, as it died, depression took its place. Many times before she had been petrified by the danger of her position, by the fear of what might happen to her if Stephen's influence was not strong enough to prevent her receiving a prison sentence. And it was strange that now, when she was so sure she could prove Maylin's guilt, she should still be filled with a nameless fear that made her body tremble as though with fever.

What was wrong? What premonition of danger made her limbs shake like this? Was it because Kim doubted there would be anything to see on the roll of film?

It was a possibility she refused to accept, and resolutely she closed her mind to it. Picking up one of the books Stephen had brought her she began to read, but the words remained a jumble in front of her eyes and irritably she flung it down.

It teetered on the edge of the bed before falling to the floor, and she was reminded of how lucky she had been the first time she had thrown the books down. If their gold wrapping paper had not caught the rays of the sun it would never have reminded her of the gold-wrapped picture frame, and she would still be sitting here without any hope whatever.

She frowned, remembering Kim's doubt. So much depended on the photograph she had taken at the General's party. Had it come out clearly enough to be recognisable?

She closed her eyes the more easily to visualise what the scene had been: The curves of the pagoda-shaped hotel roof; the sharp edges of the palm leaves; the clouds scudding away from the moon and the package in May-lin's hands suddenly glittering brightly. Moonlight had blanched it of colour, but she was sure it had been gold.

If only Kim hadn't verbalised his doubts! She sighed heavily. He more than doubted what she had said; he was certain she would never prove her belief.

"Even if you did get a shot of May-lin and the package," he'd said, *"you'd never prove it was wrapped in gold paper."*

The knowledge that he might be right did nothing to alleviate her misery. If only she had kept the original paper it might have had May-lin's fingerprints on it! If she remembered rightly she had dropped the paper on the bed and Sako had picked it up and taken it out with him, leaving her to wrap the frame in tissue paper before putting it into her own case.

She was struck again by the simple way the whole thing had been executed. May-lin had been a constant visitor to the house, and if she had been seen coming from Stephen's room, no one would have questioned her. Even if Stephen himself had found the package, once he'd seen the General's photograph he would have accepted it as a bona fide gift. Yet what would have happened if he had rung the General to thank him?

Julia frowned, unable to believe that this possibility had not been foreseen and taken care of.

Of course! General Banton had been called to an emergency meeting in Chieng Mei and had been unavailable to take calls. She must remember to tell Kim. It at least showed that even if Stephen *had* found the frame, he wouldn't have discovered – until too late – that it hadn't come from his friend.

Satisfied that she had solved the last remaining weak link, she perched on the bed again. But somehow her satisfaction was only surface deep. In the recesses of her mind a fear still lingered.

But fear of what?

Of whom?

Idly she picked up the book she had flung to the floor and ran her fingers along its edge. Was it something else Kim had said? Some other doubt he had raised? Yet he had only asked her what would have happened if Stephen had found the gold package himself.

She sighed. She and Sako were the only ones who had seen it – apart from May-lin, of course. Lots of people had seen the frame since that night, she thought wryly, but only three people had seen it wrapped up.

Only three people.

The words brought Julia to her feet. *That was it!* That was the nameless fear that had been gnawing inside her like a canker. *Only three people* had known that the picture frame had arrived as a gold-wrapped package: herself, Sako and May-lin.

Yet Kim had known. He had said so. Not once, but twice.

Heart pounding wildly against her ribs, Julia tried to remember exactly what he had said. But the fear which had lain dormant inside her was now stretching its tentacles along every nerve in her body, making coherent thought impossible. Yet she had to think coherently. She had to remember everything Kim had said.

Keep calm, she told herself. Keep calm and think carefully.

Step by painful step she went back over the past hour, trying to recollect every word spoken. But one thought lay uppermost in her mind, increasing her agitation and making calmness impossible; the knowledge that she had pleaded with Kim – had actually begged him to go to the house and get her camera and the roll of film.

But he mustn't get it. If he did, everything would be lost; herself and Stephen . . . the trade talks . . . everything she had fought so hard to save.

Clutching her arms around her as though this could prevent the shaking of her body, she forced herself to remember what Kim had said about May-lin. Once he had realised Julia was convinced she had seen the girl take a package in the grounds of the hotel, he had made no further attempt to dissuade her. All he had done was try and make her see how futile it was to believe she had succeeded in recording the scene with her camera.

"And even if you did get a shot of May-lin and the package," he had said, "you'd never be able to prove it was wrapped in gold paper."

But that hadn't been the first time he had described the package. He had done so when he had tried to make her believe that the whole idea of it being planted on Stephen was a figment of her imagination – of her desire to prove him innocent. If only she could remember exactly what he had said. He had been sarcastic, she remembered, making some remark about Stephen being in the habit of getting gold-wrapped gifts. . . . Yes, that was it. He had asked what would have happened if Stephen had gone to his room before Sako had finished packing and seen the gold-wrapped parcel for himself.

The tentacles of fear were stronger now. No longer a tiny squid lurking deep in her subconscious but an octopus reaching out to strangle her; to prevent the truth being discovered.

And how easy this would be, for only she and Kim knew about her camera and the tell-tale roll of film. Kim, the man who had said he loved her and had wanted to marry her. The man who had promised to help her. The man who knew about the gold-wrapped picture frame even though he had never seen it in its wrapping.

But he had seen it . . . because he had been the shadowy figure who had given it to May-lin!

The nameless fear that had gripped her since his departure was no longer nameless, for the name it bore was Kim. Kim.

How blind she had been not to see it before. She remembered the first time he had come to see her and the way he had pleaded with her to tell him whom she was protecting. No wonder he had known she was innocent when he knew all along who was guilty!

What would have happened if she had told him the truth then – that she was protecting Stephen? The thought sent a shiver down her spine and for the first time she thanked heaven she had known her cell was bugged. Otherwise she would have had no reason for not confiding in him.

But to-night she *had* informed him. Had emphatically stated she had found the frame in Stephen's room. By her own words she had implicated the one person she had been determined to protect. Yet she had also mentioned May-lin. Remembering this she was flooded with relief. Once to-night's tape recording was heard, Kim would be unable to hide the truth no matter how hard he tried.

But would the recording be heard? What was there to stop Kim from destroying it?

Once more she was caught by terror. Kim was a member of General Banton's staff and, as such, was known and obeyed by the prison authorities. It would be easy for him to remove the tape, edit out May-lin's name and, leaving only Stephen's, make the entire thing sound as though she had confessed that she had been protecting Stephen the whole time. As of course she had originally done!

In a frenzy she rushed to the door. "Guard!" she screamed. "I've got to talk to Mr. Brandon. Let me talk to Mr. Brandon!"

No one answered her shouts and she began to beat on the

door, knowing even as she did so that she could cry and scream as much as she liked but no one would take any notice of her to-night.

And by to-morrow it would be too late.

Even now Kim might be on his way to Mrs. Rogers' house, searching for her camera, taking out the film, unwinding it in the electric light and irretrievably destroying the sole evidence of May-lin's guilt.

Sobbing with anger and fear, she continued to pummel at the door, but gradually the hopelessness of the situation quietened her and she sank to the floor and rested her head against the wall. It was useless. There was nothing she could do except wait. Wait and know that every passing second was sounding the death-knell to all her hopes. She would never get Stephen here to-night. Never.

The dampness of the floor penetrated her body and she began to shiver. She straightened to her knees, lacking the energy to move further. Still close to the door she heard the steps of the guard and muffled voices. He was talking to one of his friends: idle conversation, for there was a laugh and the scrape of a match. Desperately she wondered what else she could do to enlist their aid; how she could convince them she had to be free.

But why waste time trying to convince them? Why not try for freedom itself?

The idea flashed into her mind so quickly that she knew it must have lain in her subconscious for a long time, and without giving herself time to think – in case thought brought the fear of failure – she clutched at her side and fell to the floor with a loud groan, sending the chair beside her crashing down as well.

Nothing happened and she groaned again, a loud cry which she kept up with slowly decreasing force until the sound became a harsh sob. Behind her a key turned in the lock and the door opened a crack to show the face of the guard. Pretending she did not see him, she lay writhing on the floor. The door opened wider and the guard beckoned to someone behind him. A second man came in and they both looked at her for a moment before the second man came forward.

"Sick?" he asked hesitantly.

"Appendix," she mumbled, still writhing in pretended agony.

He looked at her without expression and afraid he had not understood her, she said the word more clearly.

"Appendix. Appendicitis!"

She clutched at her side and groaned again, and the guard bent over her and then straightened to speak to the one still standing by the door. The command sent him hurrying away and Julia kept up her cries even when the man lifted her up and placed her as gently as he could on the bunk.

"Pain no good?" he asked sympathetically.

She nodded and he looked even more concerned, moving to the door with obvious relief as a khaki-clad man came in. Julia had never seen him before and her heart sank as he spoke to her in excellent English. To fake illness in front of an illiterate guard who could not question her was one thing; to do so before a young and obviously efficient officer was another thing entirely.

"I understand you are in pain." He said it as a statement, not a question.

"It's my appendix," she murmured, and gave a groan which even to her own ears sounded hollow. "I had an attack before – in England – the doctor warned me it might happen again."

She gave another groan, louder this time, and the man frowned.

"It is a pity you were not taken ill earlier. There is no doctor on duty here at night."

This was the best news Julia had heard, and the cry she gave now was one of relief.

"Hospital," she gasped. "There's a British nursing home. . ."

"I am afraid that it is out of the question. If you are ill you will have to go to the prison hospital."

Julia's relief vanished. If she were sent to the prison hospital she might as well have saved herself this effort, for she had as much chance of escaping from there as she did from here.

Once again the man leaned over her, but this time he put his hand on her forehead. It was hot and wet – a visible sign of her anxiety of the past half hour – and he drew back and spoke sharply to the guard.

"I have arranged for you to be taken to the hospital," he said to Julia. "We will get a stretcher for you and take you to the car."

Her spirits soared like a bird released from a cage. So the hospital wasn't in the prison! Perhaps she had a chance of escaping after all?

Still moaning, she kept her face burrowed in her arms as the guard returned with his companion and lifted her carefully on to a wooden board. Jerkily she was carried out of the cell and along the corridor to the courtyard, where a large car was revving up, a uniformed man at the wheel.

Staggering as realistically as she could, Julia let herself be helped off the stretcher and into the back of the car. She kept both hands clutched down over her side, determined to prevent any handcuffs going on them, but she need not have worried, for no one seemed concerned that she might escape, and were more intent on getting her to the hospital before she died on their hands!

She gave another groan, hoping to give the driver sufficient impetus to set the car in motion, but before he could do so, the guard who spoke a little English slid into the seat beside her, sending her hopes dashing to the ground.

Slowly the car moved forward and Julia peered through the window, wishing she knew how far away the hospital was. But even if it were on the other side of Bangkok it would not take long to get there at this time of night, and she knew she had very little time to formulate a plan of escape.

Yet what plan would work with the guard sitting almost on top of her? One slight move in the direction of the door and he would be after her in an instant. Besides, the car was going too fast. . . .

Too fast, she thought, and gave a gasp of pretended pain. "Slower, please, the bumping makes the pain worse."

The guard exclaimed angrily in Thai and the driver dropped his speed, though even so he seemed – to Julia's frightened eyes – to be doing at least thirty miles an hour.

They were moving down a wide thoroughfare with cars racing past on either side. To open the door and try and fall out here would be suicidal. But how much longer could she wait? Were they near the hospital yet? Once there and seen by a doctor, he would know immediately that her illness was false. Tears of mortification filled her eyes and she began to cry.

"Pain very bad?" the guard asked anxiously.

"Very," she mumbled.

"You like ice?"

She lifted her head and stared at him stupidly.

"I once medical orderly in Army," he explained with pride. "I see doctor put ice on man's belly. I get ice from restaurant. Small pieces in cloth . . . make pain better."

Once again he shouted to the driver and with a screech of brakes the car shuddered to a stop beside the kerb.

"I back quick," the guard said to Julia, and jumped out of the car.

She remained slunk down on the seat, wondering how best to take advantage of her good luck. If you could call it luck to have one man towering over you instead of two! She lifted her head and the driver slewed round to look at her. Dark-skinned and impassive, he stared at her with open curiosity and she gave the most heart-breaking whimper she could.

He muttered something and she repeated her cry and pointed to the door. He shook his head and, lowering it, peered out of the window at the small restaurant where they had stopped. Through its lighted windows could be seen a crowded interior, and as though to indicate they might have to wait a long time,

167

he tapped his watch and shook his head.

Knowing she had to hurry, Julia groaned and clutched dramatically at her side. "Get me some ice quickly," she cried, and pointed to the restaurant. "Ice," she said again, and gave a sharp scream of pain.

As though the scream had a point, the man jumped back in his seat, hitting his head on the roof. A spate of Thai washed over her in garlic breath, then he leaped from the car and ran across the wide pavement to the restaurant.

Without stopping to think Julia wrenched open the far-side door and flung herself out of the car.

Bent double in case the driver or guard should look out of the restaurant window and see her, she ran across to the other side of the road, narrowly missing being hit by a taxi. There were few pedestrians about and, reaching the kerb, she began to run, disregarding all direction; knowing only that she had to put as much distance as she could between herself and her captors.

CHAPTER THIRTEEN

THE pavement on which Julia found herself was wide and uneven, with intermittent lamp-posts throwing pools of light which seemed to increase the surrounding gloom rather than alleviate it. But even the shadows would not keep her hidden once her escape was realised, and she looked anxiously for a turning where she could branch off. To keep to this road was courting trouble.

A dark alley slunk away furtively on her left, and only fear of being found enabled her to plunge down it. No moonlight penetrated the blackness and she slowed her pace, fearful lest she stumble against garbage cans and give her position away. The smell of rotting vegetables and open sewers prickled her nostrils, but she kept as close to the wall as she could, frightened in case the paleness of her dress was seen by searching eyes.

Behind her came angry shouts and she pressed back into a narrow doorway, disregarding the rough wood that scratched her skin and the dampness of mouldering stone.

Something cold and furry touched her leg and she bit back a scream, but it was only a cat rubbing itself against her, and she remained motionless, hearing the guard and the driver calling to one another.

Footsteps came along the alley and in the darkness she saw a darker shape move nearer, given some form by the lamp lit street behind him. A voice called again and the dark shape stopped and answered. Unable to understand what was being said, she only knew it was a matter of seconds before she was discovered, and afraid even to press more closely into the alcove lest the rustle of her skirts gave her away, she closed her eyes to blot out the figure coming towards her as though, like an ostrich burying its head in the sand, she could avoid the Nemesis that was going to overtake her.

Again a voice called from the road and this time the approaching steps stopped with a shuffle, as though the feet were half turning. Soles scraped against gravel and the footsteps continued to move, but away from her this time, going back to the main thoroughfare.

Julia let out her breath in a long, trembling sigh, but fear still held her rigid. The two men were within earshot and could easily come back. She pressed more closely into the wall and felt the cat writhing against her leg, its purr as loud as a radar signal that might yet tell her enemies where she was.

Sweat trickled down her face, but she dared not wipe it away, and for several moments she remained motionless, eyes closed, body taut. In the distance an engine revved loudly. Was it the prison car? Was it really going or only making a pretence of moving, waiting for her to hear the sound and, believing herself safe, to come out and give her position away?

Somehow she doubted such subtlety of reasoning, and the belief spurred her to action. She could not remain here for ever. She had escaped in order to get to Mrs. Rogers' house before Kim and she had already wasted precious time.

Gingerly she stepped out into the alleyway again; then heedless of being seen, she raced down it as though the devil was at her heels.

Emerging from the blackness into a lighted road again, she paused, blinking. She did not recognise one single sign or shop and for the first time realised that though she might be free, she was as far from doing what she had set out to do as though she were still a prisoner.

Heaven alone knew in what part of Bangkok she was, and how far from Mrs. Rogers' house! Penniless, she had no hope of getting a taxi, for it would be impossible to explain to the driver that if he would help her she would pay him later. If only she had a few bahts on her to call Stephen or the British Embassy for help. By the time she reached the house it might be too late.

Even now Kim might be in possession of the camera, perhaps already destroying the film and, with it, her only chance of proving both her innocence and Stephen's.

But she mustn't think of that. She must believe she was in time. Must continue to hope . . . and pray. Dear God, don't let me be too late. Help me . . . help me. . . .

On and on she ran, pausing only when shortage of breath forced her to continue in a gasping, stumbling gait, then running again when she was able to breathe more easily. But still she saw no building she recognised and despair weighed down her feet like lead. It was hopeless. She might as well give up now. Kim had won. He and May-lin had succeeded in doing what they had planned.

Yet despair did not so easily conquer her stupid hopes, and still she kept running, too tired to think any more, knowing only that she could not stop no matter what happened.

An intersection loomed ahead of her, with cars careering round a small central island. But all the road signs were in Thai and totally incomprehensible, and she plunged to the right and hoped for the best.

The new street was busier, with several shops open despite the lateness of the hour. It seemed never-ending, stretching ahead of her like the road to Mecca. If only she could be as certain of reaching her goal as a pilgrim! Past several small cafés she went; past chattering girls walking hand in hand, displays of affection which had struck her as strange when she had first seen it, but which she now took for granted: past a large cinema with flashing neon lights and loud music pumping out into the warm, tropical night to envelop the hordes of teenagers thronging the pavement outside.

A few of them paused in their laughter to look at her as she tried to hurry by as unobtrusively as she could, and she wondered whether or not to throw herself on to the mercy of one of them and plead for help. Surely someone in this crowd spoke English? Perhaps if she explained what she wanted . . . asked for help....

But why should they help her? How could she be sure they wouldn't surround her and prevent her from escaping while they called the police?

Quickening her pace, she ran by, though the music only faded as she plunged down another alley on her left. Here too shops were open, and the smell of frying meats and rice reminded her that she had not eaten for hours. But there was no time to think about food. Other, more important things had to be done and she raced out of the alley and found herself in yet another street she did not know.

Depression rooted her to the spot. This was the end. She could go no further. Her eyes brimmed with tears and a bright red neon sign blurred and enlarged ahead of her. She blinked and the sign cleared and became readable.

Mitsubichi: name of a well-known Japanese electrical company.

Never had she thought she would welcome a sign with so much joy. Wonderful, heavenly Mitsubichi! So famous, so reliable and so near to Mrs. Rogers' house!

Unbelievably her blind stumbling had taken her in the right direction! Smoothing her hair and her dress, for several people were looking at her curiously, she began to walk purposefully along the road until the familiar high wall surrounding the garden of the house came into sight.

She quickened her pace and within a few moments had reached the gates. They were locked and her hand was raised to the bell when she drew back. It would be dangerous to call the night-watchman. Sight of her would tell him she had escaped and she did not trust him not to call the police.

She peered through the wooden slats, but was unable to see anything. The drive stretched ahead of her, dark and curving, and she had no idea whether or not Kim's car was parked in front of the house.

She began to walk again, following the wall as it curved down a narrow road lined with small trees and smelling of stagnant water: a newly reclaimed *klong*, its drainage was still imperfect and gravel crunched damply beneath her feet. On her right, set back on small patches of verdant green, were wood-framed Thai houses, perched like drunken men on stilts, their first-floor balconies covered with flowers, large pottery jars and the inevitable family of grandparents, parents and swarming children.

Once more the garden wall curved away from her and, still following it, she knew she was at the back of the house itself. If she remembered rightly there should be another gate here, leading to the houses where the servants lived, and where the night-watchman slept during the day.

If Mrs. Rogers' rule was obeyed this gate too would be locked, but remembering the lackadaisical way with which trespassing was regarded — none of the servants could understand their employer's obsession with security — she was banking on the gate having been left open.

Suddenly it was upon her and she pushed it. It remained firm and her heart gave a sickening jolt of disappointment.

Weakly she leaned against it, and as it felt her weight it creaked and seemed to move. Gingerly she pushed it again and it appeared to give way a little. The fact that it moved at all told her that the bolts which should have wedged it firmly into the ground had not been released, and she knew that only a flimsy lock was holding the two wooden gates together.

Putting both hands where she imagined the lock to be, she pushed as hard as she could. There was a loud creak of protesting wood and she looked around quickly to see if anyone had heard. But though lights glimmered dimly no one could see her and stepping back a pace, she flung herself bodily at the gates. This time they gave way with a loud splintering sound, and not pausing to draw breath she slipped between them into the garden.

Thick shrubbery masked even the faint moonlight that filtered through a cloud-filled sky and for an instant she paused to get her exact bearing. Then keeping away from any of the paths she sped across the lawn, resolutely refusing to think what would happen if she saw a snake.

The bulk of the house loomed ahead of her through the trees. It was in darkness save for a light coming from the kitchen quarters, and as she neared it she made out two people inside. Careful to make sure she was not seen, she moved closer. She recognised the man as the watchman but did not know the woman. Perhaps it was his wife? Even as she watched, he reached out and touched the brown-skinned hand that was offering him a bowl from which steam eddied. The sight of it reminded Julia of her hunger; she had not eaten since lunch-time. No wonder she was feeling faint, though it was probably as much from fear and excitement as the need for food.

If the watchman and his wife were in the kitchen there was a good chance that the back door was open, and crouching low she tiptoed towards it. The back door gave access to the pantry and from here a door led into the hall.

Cautiously she put her hand on the knob and turned it as gently as she could. It moved easily and, holding her breath, she slowly eased it open and edged her way into the pantry.

The door leading to the kitchen was open and light streamed out from it, slanting across the floor a few inches from her feet. Afraid to expel her breath, she remained stationary. The sibilant sound of conversation reassured her that her entry had not been heard, and carefully keeping her back to the wall, she inched her way along it to the furthermost door. A knob dug into her back, but she refused to turn in case the movement attracted attention, and she fumbled at the handle blindly, her breath releasing on a sigh as the door slid soundlessly open and she stepped through it into the hall.

So far, so good.

The knowledge that she had successfully reached the house and got inside it left her weak and shaking, but there was no time for triumph and she tiptoed over to peep through the narrow window set into one side of the front door.

The driveway was deserted and there was no sign of Kim's car. The relief that she had got here before him seemed to take her last vestige of energy, and she collapsed on to the nearest chair, her body shaking, her legs feeling as if they were made from cotton wool. If fear could turn hair grey, she thought inconsequentially, she would be white-haired already.

Gradually her nerves steadied and she stood up and glanced at her watch. Ten o'clock. Kim would be here soon. He might even be on his way. There was no time to waste. No time to call Stephen and tell him what had happened. She would do it in a few moments . . . as soon as she had found her camera and the film. That all-important film.

Still careful to make no sound, she sped upstairs. The long corridor stretched ahead of her, silent and deserted, chairs standing like lonely sentinels against the walls. At the far end a lighted lamp threw a window into relief, but it only heightened the blackness of the sky outside, and the panes of glass stared back at her like so many gaping, sightless eyes.

Her feet made no sound on the rugs that covered the floor as she raced down to her room. Unable to prevent her joy, she gave a soft exuberant laugh as she opened the door and went in.

Not pausing to put on the light, she ran over to the chest of drawers and opened the top one. A small sandalwood box nestled among a pile of lingerie and she lifted the lid, took out a key and hurried over to fit it into the bureau drawer. It turned smoothly and the door slid open. Putting her hand inside, she withdrew her camera.

Only now could she afford to savour the pleasure of success and she stared at the six square inches of leather and metal in her hands. So ordinary-looking yet so important, not only to her and Stephen but to the success and prosperity of Thailand.

Quickly she opened the camera case and began rewinding the spool. Her fingers shook so much that it took her twice as long as normal, but eventually she felt the spool tighten and, pressing the release catch, undid the base of the camera and took out the film.

It lay smooth as silk in her palm, weighing no more than a few ounces yet able to tip the balance between the success or failure of the trade talks. Calmness descended on her, yet her heart would not steady and pounded so heavily against her ribs that she found it difficult to breathe. She took a gulp of air and expelled it slowly, hearing it rasp in her ears. She took another breath, but this time the rasping sound did not match the rise and fall of her chest and with a sickening sense of fear she knew what was wrong.

Someone else was breathing in the room.

The hair on her scalp tingled and she felt a prickle of sweat between her breasts. Clutching the film tight, she forced herself to turn and raise her eyes, knowing as she did so whom she would see.

Kim.

"Hello, Julia," he said easily. "I was told you had escaped."

"The opportunity came along," she said with masterly understatement, "and I took it."

"That wasn't quite the story I heard!"

"How did – how did you find out?"

"I rang the prison before coming here. I don't know why I did – Fate, I suppose."

"Fate," she echoed, and hoped her voice did not hold the bitterness she felt. "You once tried to make *me* believe in it."

"But you wouldn't."

"I do now," she said staunchly, "otherwise I'd never have managed to escape!"

Her remark brought no smile, but she refused to let it deter her. She had to pretend innocence and ignorance. It was her only chance of coming out of this alive.

"It was very clever of you to find me!" she added ingenuously. "How did you guess I'd come here?"

"It was the obvious thing for you to do." He held out his

hand. "The film, Julia."

"You won't need it now. I'll get Stephen to develop it."

"I can have it done more quickly."

"Do you have contacts too?" she asked lightly. "I sometimes think life in Bangkok would grind to a halt if no one had any contacts!"

"The film, Julia," Kim repeated.

Pretending she hadn't heard him, she chattered on. "I daresay Stephen'll be here any minute. I left word at his hotel to say I was coming here. He should have got it by now."

"You didn't leave any message." Kim was still smiling, still speaking in the same gentle voice. So obviously in command of the situation that Julia could barely control her panic.

"I checked his hotel at the same time I telephoned the prison," Kim went on. "They said he'd gone to Pattaya. I believe he's with May-lin and Mrs. Rogers. All your friends are in Pattaya, Julia. You're alone in Bangkok."

"Don't make it sound so ominous," she said gaily. "I've got *you!*"

"Of course. So let me help you. That was the intention, wasn't it? That I should develop the film for you?" His smile was wider now and infinitely more frightening. "Come, my dear, stop prevaricating and give me the film."

"No!" Gone was the time for pretence. Kim was playing with her like a cat with a mouse and she was tired of it. "No," she cried again. "I won't give it to you."

With a sudden sharp movement she turned and flung the film to the furthest corner of the room, where bureau, chairs and table were clustered together.

"That was a silly thing to do," he commented quietly. "All you've done is gain an extra few minutes. Now go over and find it."

"Find it yourself!" Defiantly she glared at him. "I know what you are – what you did! You're in it with May-lin. You were the man in the hotel garden – the one who gave her the

177

picture frame."

"Yes, my dear. Yes to everything you've said." His head tilted to one side and the smile left his face, making it look troubled and sad. "When I heard you'd escaped, I wondered if you had guessed the truth. I'm sorry you have. Very sorry. I tried so hard not to give myself away. I don't know how I did!"

She remained silent and he came a step closer. "What did I say? What did I do?" Still she said nothing and he repeated the question. "Answer me, Julia. I want to know where I went wrong. . . . I don't want to make the same mistake again."

The meaning in his words turned her blood to ice and she shivered.

"Gold paper," she replied. "You knew the frame had been wrapped in gold paper." He looked puzzled and she explained: "No one had seen it wrapped up except Sako and myself and May-lin and the man who'd given it to her."

Kim sighed. "That was stupid of me. But then I have always been stupid where you were concerned. Whenever I am near you I'm not in control of myself."

"Spare me that," she said rudely. "You needn't pretend any more."

"I never pretended about loving you. I meant it."

She was surprised. "You mean you would have married me?"

"I asked you to be my wife," he replied, as if that answered her question. "If only you hadn't interfered in this!" he burst out, suddenly angry. "Why did you have to take the frame that night? And when you saw what was in it, why couldn't you have admitted it wasn't yours?"

"Because I wanted to protect Stephen!"

"Ah yes. The trade talks."

"Not only that," she said tightly, "but because I love him."

For a moment Kim was silent, and watching him she knew she had said the one thing calculated to hurt him most.

"Did you never care for me?" he asked at last.

"I liked you," she admitted. "Very much, as a matter of

fact. But I never loved you."

"I see." He braced his shoulders. "It seems we have both wasted our love. You will never have Stephen and I will never have you."

"What are you going to do?"

"The only thing I *can* do. Destroy the film and . . ." he hesitated, "and you too, I'm afraid."

"You'll never get away with it!"

"I already have. In a few minutes it will be over. By running away from prison you've made everything much easier. I came here because I was certain this was where you'd make for. You tried to shoot me, but I – I fought to get the gun away from you and while doing so it went off. A most regrettable accident," he shrugged. "But an accident nonetheless."

He moved to the centre of the room and for the first time she saw the thing glinting in his hand. Dark, stubby, pointing at her as casually as an unlit cigar.

Only then did the full horror of her position strike her. This was no game she was playing but a battle of life or death. No, she amended wearily, not a battle, for the very word implied a doubt about the outcome. And there was no doubt what this outcome would be. In this large cool bedroom where she had lain so many nights and thought of Stephen, she would lie finally without any thought at all.

"You're going to kill me," she said dully.

"I have no choice. I would give anything not to have to do it, but –"

"Then don't. It isn't too late to –"

"It's far too late, Julia." His face was pale. "Much as I love you, I love my country more!"

"Is that why you want to destroy it?"

"I'm saving it! Do you think I want to see us tied to Europe's apron strings for ever? We want our freedom, the right to develop in our own way and at our own pace. We've been lackeys to the white man long enough."

"You're out of your mind!"

"Because I see our future with other Far East countries?"

"Because you see it with the Communists! What sort of freedom do you think Thailand will have with *them*?"

"More freedom than if it is controlled by European companies."

It was a point of view she had heard Stephen discuss with another diplomat. But hearing Kim say the same words gave them a newer, more dangerous meaning. Here was ideology gone mad; loyalty turned to fanaticism with all the violence and evil that this implied.

"We would have been so happy together," Kim was saying, and the sadness of his voice was more menacing than his anger had been.

"Don't do it," she pleaded, "don't kill me."

"You leave me no choice." His eyes narrowed as though in pain, his hand shook and his finger tightened.

"No!" she screamed, and the sound clashed with the sharp sound of a shot.

She gasped and swayed, the acrid smell of cordite in her nostrils, the bitter taste of fear in her mouth.

But she was alive . . . unharmed. . . .

Disbelieving, she flung out her arms and felt them caught in a tight, bone-shattering grip.

"Thank God you're safe!" It was Stephen's voice in her ears. Stephen's face staring into her own. But a face she had never seen before: lined and sunken, colourless and sweating.

Her eyes moved away from him and rested on the floor. Kim lay there writhing in pain, his hand, shattered and bloody, no longer holding a gun. As she watched, two men in uniform pulled him to his feet and led him out.

"It's like a ghastly version of that proverb," she whispered looking at Stephen again.

"What proverb?"

"About an eye for an eye," she said in a high, toneless voice.

"Only this one's different – it was a hand for a life. Except that it wasn't a hand any more," she said huskily, and fainted.

It seemed a long time later that she awoke to find herself lying on the settee in the living room, with Stephen leaning against the arm and Mrs. Rogers hovering close by and unexpectedly looking her age.

"So you've finally come round," Mrs. Rogers said with relief. "I thought you were going to make a night of it!"

"I nearly made a *life* of it!" Julia replied with a shaky laugh. "If Stephen hadn't arrived. . . ." She looked at him and seeing Julia's expression, Mrs. Rogers marched to the door.

"I'll go and see about some food for us. I don't know about you two, but I'm starving!"

Alone with Stephen, Julia felt a surge of embarrassment and, unable to meet his eyes, made a pretence of needing to rest back on the cushions. Yet the urge to know what had brought them to the house so opportunely conquered her shyness enough for her to speak.

"How did you know I'd escaped?" she asked. "And that I'd be here?"

He hesitated and then said abruptly: "I'm sure you knew the mood I was in when I left you earlier to-day? When I first left Thailand I was certain you were protecting Nick – that he'd put marijuana in the frame without telling you. It wasn't until I saw him. . . ."

Stephen's voice grew deeper, as though he found it difficult to control his emotion, though she wasn't sure whether it was emotion born of anger or fear of what might have happened to her.

"After he got your wire in Hamburg he flew straight back to see me and practically threatened murder unless I came back here and saved you! I told him *he* was the only one who could do that and – " Stephen paused, "I'm sure you can guess the rest. Nick swore he knew nothing about the picture frame *or* the marijuana. That's when I decided to get the next plane here."

"I'm surprised you believed him."

"Judging people is part of my business," came the dry answer. "Though I wasn't very successful when it came to *you*!"

"So you flew back here after seeing Nick," she said quickly.

"Yes. I was sure I could clear everything up as soon as I'd talked to you. Unfortunately everything you said made it worse. You kept saying you were protecting someone and I naturally assumed it was Kim." A faint smile, not an amused one because the danger that had surrounded Julia was still too near for him to feel any amusement, lifted the corners of his mouth. "When you think over the conversation we had, you'll realise it was like cross-talk between a couple of comedians – except that it wasn't funny. I misunderstood everything you said."

"I thought I was being so clear," she said shakily.

"So clear that all I wanted was to murder Kim! When I left you this afternoon I was all set to go after him."

"But you didn't?"

"Logic came to my rescue," he said wryly. "I decided to tell the General everything I'd found out and see if there were some way we could bluff Kim into admitting his guilt."

"But why did you think Kim wanted me to smuggle marijuana?"

"Because of its value. I knew he wanted to marry you and I assumed his family didn't approve. I thought he was trying to get enough money out of the country so that he could live with you abroad."

Julia digested this remark while Stephen stood up and went to stand by the window.

"His family didn't disapprove," she said at last. "There was never any problem about that."

"I realise that now, but this morning when I left you. . . ."

"How did you finally work out the truth?" she asked.

"I didn't." He gave a short bark of unamused laughter. "I was in no mood to work out anything. I was so furious with you. . . ." He turned away from the window but remained beside it, his hands gripping the back of a chair so tightly that his knuckles showed white. "I was on my way to see the General when Mrs. Rogers passed me in her car. She was going to Pattaya. She hadn't known I'd come back to Thailand and she set her chauffeur chasing after me. She finally caught up with me and I was forced to stop. I was in no mood to chat, but when she found out I'd seen you she insisted on knowing what had happened. I told her you said you were protecting the man you loved and that I was going to see if the General could pressurise Kim into admitting the truth." He paused and for the first time looked hesitant. "What Mrs. Rogers actually said to that is something I'll leave to your imagination. But the gist of it was that I was a damn fool if I didn't know the man you loved was *me*! Once she'd got that to sink in, a lot of things began to make sense and I knew I had to see you again. By the time I got back to the prison you'd already escaped."

"But what led you here?" Julia had to ask the question though she was still careful to avoid meeting his eyes. "Surely this was the last place I'd have come to if I didn't want to be caught."

Even though she refused to look at him, the jerkiness of his voice gave away his tension. "That's where luck played its part," he said tightly. "*I* thought you'd make for the British Embassy and Mrs. Rogers thought you'd try to get to *her* in Pattaya. We'd just decided to try the Embassy when one of the warders suggested we spoke to Major Chan – as he'd been the last person to talk to you. I don't know why, but I had the feeling it was important to hear exactly what you'd said to him. I knew our conversation had been taped and I was pretty sure the same applied to anyone else you spoke to."

Stephen stopped, as though memory made it too painful for him to go on, but after a moment he continued, speaking in the same tight, controlled manner. "I tried to persuade the senior warder to let me hear a playback of your conversation with Kim, but it wasn't till I contacted the General that I was able to do so.

Once I did. everything became clear . . ."

"You heard Kim talk about the gold paper?"

He nodded. "I had to play it back several times before I realised how he gave himself away. Once I knew, it was easy to guess you'd come here to get the roll of film before he did. Then it was just a question of getting here in time."

"*Just,*" she said shakily.

"What a word," he replied, his tone ragged. "I hope I never cut things so fine again."

"So do I," she replied, and resting her head on the brocaded settee again, closed her eyes.

Though she could not see Stephen she was aware of his every movement; of him crossing the carpet to come and stand close beside her; of the aroma of cigar that emanated from him and the unexpected warmth and tenderness in his voice when he spoke.

"I suppose Mrs. Rogers *was* right?" he asked quietly.

"About what?"

"About your protecting me?"

Julia swallowed. "I thought a scandal would – would harm the trade talks."

"You carried loyalty to your country very far."

"You would have done the same in my position."

"Was it only loyalty?"

"Yes."

"You're lying!"

His words were so impassioned that her eyes flew open, and only as she saw his face, still colourless beneath its tan, did she know how deeply disturbed he still was. The knowledge of how closely she had come to death – that she would already be dead if he had not burst into the bedroom when he did – made her pride seem a poor and feeble thing. What did it matter if Stephen knew she loved him?

"You're right," she said shakily. "I *am* lying. I didn't do it because of the Delegation. I did it because – because I . . . . You *know* why," she whispered.

"I'd like you to explain more clearly," he said in the politest of tones. "Why did you think I'd *want* to smuggle anything out of Thailand?"

"Because of what you said about needing excitement – about pitting your wits against authority . . . putting yourself in danger. Those are the exact words you used – here in this room!"

"I might enjoy taking risks," Stephen replied, folding his arms across his chest, "but I wouldn't resort to a damn fool thing like smuggling – and certainly not drugs! How could you think I would!"

"I don't know," she said miserably. "At the time it seemed so – so logical. . . . I'm sorry."

"Sorry!" As though the word were a spring releasing him, he knelt down and gripped her hands. "Sorry for trying to protect me? For allowing yourself to be kept in prison for weeks? My God, Julia, if anyone should be sorry, it's *me*!" He peered into her face, his drawl dispersed by remorse, by the torrent of emotion that was visible in the way his fingers were digging into her flesh.

"There's so much I want to say to you," he burst out, "that I don't know where to begin."

"I don't want you to thank me. There's no need for that."

"I agree." Her words seemed to check his emotion and he was again in command of himself. "What I feel for you goes far beyond thanks." Releasing her, he stood up, but he remained beside her, his hand lightly touching her hair. Lifting up one dark red strand, he let it run through his fingers. "You left me in England because I hadn't known what colour it was," he murmured, "but you didn't realise there were many things about you I *had* noticed. Your warmth and sympathy; your ability to know what was in my mind before I knew it myself. I was beginning to trust you more than any other woman I'd met – beginning to think you were the one person who could – He stopped and flung out his hands. " When you said you wanted to get another job, I thought you were trying to tell me you didn't care for me – that you only saw me as your employer."

"You'd never been anything else," she said quietly. "You were very adept at hiding your feelings."

"Because I was only beginning to realise them myself! By the time I had, you'd told me you were going."

"Why didn't you give me a hint?" she asked curiously.

"Would you have believed me? You were so angry with me by then you'd have thought I was making it up in order not to lose a good secretary!"

"That wouldn't have been my *only* reason for doubting you," she said dryly. "There was May-lin too."

He caught his breath. "Ah, yes . . . well, I never professed to be a monk." There was a short silence. "When I found myself thinking so much about you," he admitted, "I tried to put up a fight."

"It was a good one," she said with a slight smile. "And you used *me* to order your flowers and scent!"

"I thought it might spark off your jealousy," he retorted, "but you never gave a sign of it. Sometimes I wondered if there was ice in your veins instead of blood!" He paused as though waiting for her to say something and when she remained silent he moved back a step to look more clearly into her face. "Something else is on your mind, isn't it?"

She hesitated and then decided to go on being honest. "I was wondering what would have happened if you hadn't come to Thailand. I mean, we – we might never have met again."

"I'd already made arrangements to come here and see you," he said evenly, "when the Prime Minister asked me to head the Delegation."

His words sent joy coursing through her veins, but still she was afraid to give rein to it and, aware of it, Stephen tilted her head and forced her to look into his eyes.

"Once I knew how I felt about you, I was determined to come here and make you fall in love with me," he said huskily. "When my secretary fell ill and Mrs. Rogers suggested you took her place, it seemed that fate was playing into my hands."

"You hid your feelings very well."

"Because I was afraid of you."

"But why?"

"Because when I last saw you in London you were a simple, unsophisticated girl and when I saw you here you were a swan!" He glared at her. "If I'd suddenly told you I loved you, you'd have thought it was sexual attraction!"

"Wasn't it?" she asked demurely.

"You know very well that it wasn't." He drew her up and rested his cheek against hers. "I love the way you look now," he said softly, "but I loved you just as much before. I loved *you*. The way you thought, the way you acted . . . everything that makes you the person you are."

The unsteadiness in his voice grew and he stopped speaking, but he still remained close, his hands lightly clasping her waist. "Those first weeks after you left me were hell. I kept remembering everything you'd said, everything you'd accused me of, and I knew how right you were and how blind I'd been." He lifted his head and looked into her eyes. "I might not be seeing too clearly yet, but if you're willing to help me . . . I love you, Julia! Do you know what I'm trying to say?"

"I think so." Slowly, tentatively, she put her arms around his neck. But though she longed to accept the assurance of his words she was unable to do so.

"What else is worrying you?" he asked quietly. "I know there's something on your mind."

"It's nothing – nothing important."

"You once said real love only comes with understanding. If you mean that, you won't lie to me."

She half turned away from him, knowing he was right to persist in his questioning, yet knowing that once she answered him she would be giving herself away completely.

"Tell me, Julia," he said again. "Tell me."

"It's May-lin. It's silly of me, I know, but I – I keep remembering the week-end you spent with her in Pattaya."

"I stayed in her house," he said quietly, "but I wasn't her lover." Though he heard Julia catch her breath, he ignored it and went on speaking. "From the moment I knew how I felt about you, I wasn't able to – I never even *wanted* another woman! It was you or no one." His voice grew sharper, more authoritative. "If May-lin said anything to the contrary she was lying!"

Listening to him Julia did not doubt his truthfulness, and jealousy of May-lin vanished as though it had never existed. There were many things she and Stephen would have to talk about, but for the moment the most important thing was that they were together – that their future lay with each other.

With a little murmur she came to rest in his arms and feeling his trembling body, knowing she was the cause of it, her confidence grew and she twined her arms around him and pulled him tightly against her.

"I'll never mention May-lin again," she whispered.

"Not even to ask where she is now?"

Julia's eyes widened and she gave an exclamation. "I'd forgotten what she'd done. All I could think of was what she might have meant to you!"

"That's a satisfactory answer for my ego," he smiled, "but I'll tell you even so. Then we needn't discuss her again." He paused, his eyes suddenly brooding. "When I think she was willing to let you sacrifice yourself...."

"Don't." Julia put her hands on his cheek. "All that's over now. Just tell me what's happened to her."

"She left the country yesterday. I have a feeling she was worried something might leak out. Anyway, she took herself off for a so-called holiday to South America."

"South America!"

"She won't stay there long. I rather think she'll make for China. She knows she can never come back here. Not while the

188

present government are in power anyway." Stephen tightened his arms round Julia's waist. "Now that's finished May-lin for us. Let's talk about you instead. I take it you do love me? You haven't actually said so."

"Do I need to put it into words?"

"Or deeds," he replied unsteadily. "I think I'd prefer deeds."

For answer she raised her hands and cupped them either side of his face, then gently pulled his head down until his lips were resting on hers. For an instant their pressure remained light, then they grew harder, demanding, forcing her to a response that robbed her of coherent thought. Her mouth moved under his, showing him the best way she could that her surrender was complete. His body trembled as though with fever and his hands were warm through the thin silk of her dress, growing warmer as they undid the buttons of her bodice and caressed the soft curves of her breast.

Convulsively she pressed herself closer to him, the pounding of her heart matching his as his fingers moved along the base of her spine.

"Stephen!" she gasped. "I love you . . . so much. . . ."

"Darling. . . ."

Unexpectedly he drew back, his hands pushing her away from him. "No," he said shakily. "I daren't go on holding you. I'm only human and. . . ." He stopped speaking and moved slightly back, his eyes narrowing. "You won't start playing hard to get, will you?"

"How can I? You already have me!"

"Not quite! That's what I mean, actually. I want to marry you soon. The minute I can get a licence. I know you have your work, but – "

"You come first," she said quickly. "I'd like to go on with my photography, but there'll be plenty of scope in England."

"You can travel abroad if you wish," he said quietly. "I won't stand in your way."

She stared at him, knowing full well what an effort it must

have cost him to say these words.

"Thank you, Stephen. But I don't think I'll ever feel so strongly about my work that I'll want to go away without you. I'm sure I'll be able to combine my travelling to fit in with yours."

His face was transfigured with tenderness, but still he refused to be dissuaded. "I mean it, Julia. I'll try not to be possessive about you. You have your own life and a talent. If you want to use it – "

"My main talent lies in being your wife and making you happy. I haven't the same ability or drive that your mother had, my darling, but I'm glad you made the offer anyway."

Not giving him a chance to reply, she ran into his arms again and nestled close against him. "No more words," she whispered. "Just actions."

"Actions," he echoed, and placed his mouth on hers. "The licence first," he breathed huskily, "and then you'll have all the action you want!"

FREE!
Harlequin Romance Catalogue

Here is a wonderful opportunity to read many of the Harlequin Romances you may have missed.

The HARLEQUIN ROMANCE CATALOGUE lists hundreds of titles which possibly are no longer available at your local bookseller. To receive your copy, just fill out the coupon below, mail it to us, and we'll rush your catalogue to you!

Following this page you'll find a sampling of a few of the Harlequin Romances listed in the catalogue. Should you wish to order any of these immediately, kindly check the titles desired and mail with coupon.

Have You Missed Any of These

Harlequin Romances?

☐ 732 RIVER NURSE, Joyce Dingwell
☐ 737 MAIDEN FLIGHT, Betty Beaty
☐ 744 VERENA FAYRE, PROBA-
     TIONER, Valerie K. Nelson
☐ 745 TENDER NURSE, Hilda Nickson
☐ 746 LOYAL IN ALL, Mary Burchell
     (Original Harlequin title
     "Nurse Marika, Loyal in
     All")
☐ 748 THE VALLEY OF PALMS
     Jean S. Macleod
☐ 754 THE RANCHER NEEDS A WIFE
     Celine Conway
☐ 764 NURSE ANN WOOD
     Valerie K. Nelson
☐ 771 NURSE PRUE IN CEYLON
     Gladys Fullbrook
☐ 787 THE TWO FACES OF NURSE
     ROBERTS   Nora Sanderson
☐ 790 SOUTH TO THE SUN
     Betty Beaty
☐ 794 SURGEON'S RETURN
     Hilda Nickson
☐ 939 DOCTOR'S DAUGHTER
     Jean S. Macleod
☐ 945 DOCTOR SANDY
     Margaret Malcolm
☐ 951 THE ENCHANTED TRAP
     Kate Starr
☐ 952 A COTTAGE IN SPAIN
     Rosalind Brett
☐ 972 BARBARY MOON
     Kathryn Blair
☐ 993 SEND FOR NURSE ALISON
     Marjorie Norrell
☐ 994 JUBILEE HOSPITAL
     Jan Tempest
☐ 995 NURSE RONNIE'S VOCATION
     Felicity Hayle
☐ 1001 NO PLACE FOR SURGEONS
     Elizabeth Gilzean
☐ 1009 NURSE AT FAIRCHILDS
     Marjorie Norrell
☐ 1044 PARADISE ISLAND
     Hilary Wilde
☐ 1063 THE MAN FROM RHODESIA
     Ruth Clemence
☐ 1064 MISTRESS OF THE HOUSE
     Eleanor Farnes

☐ 1065 STUDENT NURSE AT SWALE
     Pauline Ash
☐ 1067 TERRACE IN THE SUN
     Anne Weale
☐ 1068 THE DUTCH UNCLE
     Margery Hilton
☐ 1069 THE MAN FROM THE VALLEY
     Joyce Dingwell
☐ 1070 THE DRUMMER OF CORRAE
     Jean S. Macleod
☐ 1602 REMEDY FOR LOVE
     Flora Kidd
☐ 1603 RING OF JADE   Margaret Way
☐ 1604 THAT MAN NEXT DOOR
     Lucy Gillen
☐ 1606 THE QUIET VELD, Jean Dunbar
☐ 1607 NOT LESS THAN ALL
     Margaret Malcolm
☐ 1608 VINEYARD IN A VALLEY
     Gloria Bevan
☐ 1610 DEAR CONQUISTADOR
     Margery Hilton
☐ 1612 MISTRESS OF ELVAN HALL
     Mary Cummins
☐ 1613 MOMENT OF DECISION
     Jean S. Macleod
☐ 1615 A THOUSAND CANDLES
     Joyce Dingwell
☐ 1659 A PARADE OF PEACOCKS
     Elizabeth Ashton
☐ 1660 A STRANGER CAME
     Jane Donnelly
☐ 1661 OLIVE ISLAND   Kay Thorpe
☐ 1662 A SERPENT IN EDEN
     Eleanor Farnes
☐ 1663 THE CAVE OF THE WHITE
     ROSE   Flora Kidd
☐ 1700 GONE BEFORE MORNING
     Lilian Peake
☐ 1744 WINTER LOVING Janice Gray
☐ 1745 NURSE AT NOONGWALLA
     Roumelia Lane
☐ 1746 WITHOUT ANY AMAZEMENT
     Margaret Malcolm
☐ 1747 THE FIELDS OF HEAVEN
     Anne Weale
☐ 1748 THE GOLDEN MADONNA
     Rebecca Stratton
☐ 1749 LOVELY IS THE ROSE
     Belinda Dell

All books are 60c. Please use the handy order coupon.

B